# Checkers on the Hill

DORIS WILBUR

MILFORD
HOUSE
an imprint of Sunbury Press, Inc.
Mechanicsburg, PA USA

## MILFORD HOUSE

an imprint of Sunbury Press, Inc.
Mechanicsburg, PA USA

For information about special discounts for bulk purchases, please contact Sunbury Press Orders Dept. at (855) 338-8359 or orders@sunburypress.com.

To request one of our authors for speaking engagements or book signings, please contact Sunbury Press Publicity Dept. at publicity@sunburypress.com.

FIRST MILFORD HOUSE PRESS EDITION: January 2023

Set in Adobe Garamond Pro | Interior design by Crystal Devine | Cover by Lawrence Knorr | Cover art by Doris Wilbur | Edited by Sarah Peachey.

Publisher's Cataloging-in-Publication Data
Names: Wilbur, Doris, author.
Title: Checkers on the hill / Doris Wilbur.
Description: First trade paperback edition. | Mechanicsburg, PA : Milford House Press, 2023.
Summary: Set among actual historical events of 1968-1969, Samuel and Josey have taken jobs in Washington, DC, an exciting, multicultural city. It is also a festering laboratory for protests, social change, violence, and deception. Josey uncovers alarming secret information at work that she cannot disclose. The secret endangers thousands, including her own family. Tough choices must be made: run back home, or stay? What would you have done?
Identifiers: ISBN : 979-8-88819-033-3 (softcover) | 979-8-88819-034-0 (ePub).
Subjects: FICTION / Family Life / General | FICTION / Historical / General | FICTION / Political.

Product of the United States of America
0 1 1 2 3 5 8 13 21 34 55

*Continue the Enlightenment!*

BASED ON A TRUE STORY

*

Dedicated to all who choose that fork in the road.

*

The dialogue of some of the characters accurately reflects the
conflicting beliefs and social norms of the story's setting
and may be disturbing.

## Chapter 1

### Hillside Farm 1954

"Did you get enough this time?" I asked my older brother as he walked toward me with handfuls of discarded bottle caps.

"Yeah, but I have to straighten 'em." Karl put a bent cap on the top of a stump we used for splitting wood and killing the chickens when we had to. Then he took a rounded stick that fit exactly right inside the crimped edges and hit the end of it with the hammer. "There, fixed it," he said and, satisfied, he held it out on his hand. The cap looked good as new.

We needed those caps for checkers. Karl's job had been to collect all the Rolling Rock beer caps Dad tossed away in the house, around the yard, and in the barn as he drank his favorite beverage. On balmy days like this, when the air hung heavy and humid and there was no hint whatsoever of a summer breeze, Dad popped a lot of those caps.

Karl was six years older than me. There were other siblings with whom he could play checkers. Most of them were a lot smarter than me and would have given him competition in the game. We all got along well most of the time, but I think he liked that, being older and smarter, he could easily beat me at any game, especially checkers.

We needed a checkerboard, so I had studied the one at school our teacher let us take out at recess time. There were sixty-four squares total. I took measurements of the outside of the board and jotted down the size of the squares. Mom had some old white muslin she let me have, and I used my wooden ruler to carefully mark out all the squares properly. Then I drew lines like a big tic-tac-toe game and colored in every other box with my black Crayola, used so much it got soft and bent in my hand.

Karl got a small paint brush and painted twelve of the metal beer caps with some red barn paint leftover from painting the outhouse earlier in the summer. That old outhouse sure did need fixing up. It was getting shabby looking, and even the leaves of vines sticking inside through the cracks between the aged gray boards did not improve its appearance. The other twelve caps left had the words Rolling Rock written in silver across the blue top. We set up our game on the shady side porch of the house. It was screened from the annoying, buzzing insects and was out of the hot summer sun. The red barn paint dried quickly, and soon we were ready to play. Karl went over the rules of the game.

"Now put your checkers on the black squares closest to you, not on the white ones," he said. "You should have three rows of them."

"I know. I know how to do this," I told him. I had played the game in school, but he insisted on going over all the rules as if he was the master and only authority on how to play. He put his Rolling Rocks on the three rows nearest him and kept telling me what to do. "Now, you can only move corner to corner on an empty black square. You can't move to a white square, and you can't jump over a white square, remember that." He repeated, "It's a rule, you can't move to a white square, and you can't jump over a white square, you got that?"

"Yup," I answered, nodding my head and getting impatient. "Now, can we play?"

"Well, there's more. I'll tell you about kings when we get that far."

"Can I go first?" I asked with my hand already hovering over my red cap.

"No, Rolling Rock always goes first." He quickly grabbed a checker and moved it one square to the right. "Now, you can go."

I moved my red checker diagonally to a black square. We continued in that manner, one checker at a time, getting closer to each other with every move. Soon our checkers were almost at the center of the board.

Suddenly he barked, "Look at where your checker is!" I hadn't noticed anything wrong. "Your checker isn't sitting all the way on the black square. Look at it," he said, pointing to my red cap. "It's halfway on the white and halfway on the black. It can't be that way. It has to be *ALL* the way on the black. Get it back into its place where it belongs."

I quickly adjusted my checker, wanting to make my brother happy and play the game according to the rules. Now, my checker was resting correctly within the boundaries of its black square. We continued playing. He captured some of my checkers and I got a few of his. I was getting close to jumping another of his Rolling Rocks when he yelled at me again.

"You did the same thing. Your checker is half on the black and half on the white. I don't know where it's supposed to be. Are you trying to cheat?" he asked me, leaning in and pushing his face close to mine.

"No, I'm not trying to cheat, and stop hollering at me!" I told him. "You don't know everything!" Then, looking at the board, I saw another move, used the chance, and jumped his Rolling Rock. Satisfied, I straightened my back, sat up tall, and grinned ear to ear at him. He scowled back at me. Then he saw a move, jumped over one of my red checkers, and glared right back, wrinkling his nose.

Soon we reached the time to king a playing piece, and Karl went over the rules. "A king can move in any direction," he said. "He can move left, right, forward, or back." Perhaps it was my strong ability to visualize the game that gave me an advantage. Soon, I was capturing more of his Rolling Rocks than he was getting my reds. I was going to win, and my older brother knew that. Suddenly, he shouted, "You did it again, you little turd! Look at your red checker. It's almost all on the white square! I'll repeat. It-has-to-stay-all-the-way-on-the-black-it-can't-be-on-the-white," he said very slowly. "What are you, dumb or what? I told you too many times already what the rules are. I quit!" With that, he swept his arm across the checkerboard, scattering checkers everywhere, and stormed off, mumbling, "You little turd" again.

After he left, I picked up all the caps and bundled them inside the cloth checkerboard I was so proud of making. We would play checkers another day. My brother did not stay angry long and there would be another chance to beat him.

When Karl was seventeen, right after our parents divorced, he joined the navy, then later married and left New York State to live near the San Diego naval base, where he had been stationed during his service. He raised his family there. Time passed, and we lost touch with each other.

* * *

## On Another Hill 1967

"Mom . . . Mom . . . it's your turn!" my daughter, Grace, said while shaking my arm. It brought me out of my mental wandering and back to the game of checkers I was now playing with her.

"Oh, I'm sorry, honey. I was thinking of a time I played checkers with my brother, Karl. I'm having trouble concentrating today. Did you beat me yet?"

"No, not yet, but I'm going to!" she said, grinning confidently from ear to ear.

"I bet you will," I told her. Then, realizing my mind was too distracted to focus, I asked, "Can we please finish this game later? We'll leave everything right here in place. Why don't you watch the Mickey Mouse Club while Daddy rests?"

"Okay, if you promise we can finish the game after supper," she told me and left the table to watch the show already playing.

Samuel sat slumped in a chair, half-awake. He was tired from a busy day at work.

I touched his shoulder. "Hon, will you keep an eye on things while I take a walk?"

He gave me a sleepy nod. "Sure, I can do that."

"You really have to stay awake now . . . okay?" I told him.

"I will, don't worry," he answered.

I left to go outside. The jingle for the children's television show was playing in my head: "*Who's the leader of the club that's made for you and me? M-I-C-K-E-Y--M-O-U-S-E . . . Hey There, Hi There, Ho There. You're as welcome as can be . . .*" Not wanting to keep repeating that jingle, I shook my head, trying to focus. It was late afternoon, and I needed to take a walk and think clearly. I headed toward the big field on our hillside just past the boundary where our mowed lawn gave way to wild field. We had built our home on seven acres there, and our house was surrounded by old, overgrown pastures and long hedgerows.

As I walked, the breeze that gently moved my hair carried the scent of wild ripe strawberries and timothy hay ready to cut and bale. It was a late June afternoon, and the sun was warm on my face. I felt like twirling around and singing as Julie Andrews had done in *The Sound of Music*. But I had too much on my mind for singing or dancing. Decisions were weighing heavy on my shoulders.

This land was my country world, the fields, the woods, the tall, rounded green hills surrounding me, with a ceiling of clear cerulean sky above. My home looked much smaller now that I had walked far away from it into the field. I looked toward Lester's hill across the valley. There, high on the top, between an opening in the trees, I could see the small silhouette of his two-story farmhouse with its peeling white paint, his big, old gray barn, and a cluster of haphazard outbuildings. I heard the sound of his small herd of sheep baaing to each other and wondered if Lucy was one that I now heard calling.

We had talked Lester into selling us a pregnant ewe we named Lucy. I wanted to start my own flock, but after relocating her, Lucy wasn't happy away from her home and everything familiar. She was homesick, very homesick. Soon after we got her, she broke through our barbed wire fence, ran down the steep hill, crossed the winding creek at the bottom of the valley, and traveled up through the thick evergreen woods to get back to Lester's farm and flock. Samuel and I drove all the way round on the dirt road to Lester's place. We sorted Lucy out of his flock again and fetched her back home in the truck. On the way back, Samuel said, "Josey, I don't think this ewe wants to live on our place. Sheep like to be with others of their own kind." He was right. Lucy ran away again just a few days later. She was too lonely for Lester's flock.

Looking around, I thought it would be tough for me to leave my familiar surroundings too. I gazed at the hedgerows of trees lining the borders of our fields. Gray stone walls, built decades ago, had divided those fields into areas for crops and pastures. Rabbits and other small animals were secreted away in fur-lined nests among those rocks, bushes, and trees, and raised their litters of young. I thought of the robins I looked forward to returning each March. They often came back before the snow fell for the last time, and we would see them hopping around in a late blizzard. Bluebirds, sparrows, and orioles built their nests in the trees in those hedgerows as well. Other animals, like toads and frogs, salamanders, chipmunks, and anything looking for shelter lived there too. During springtime, clouds of white blossoms covered the Juneberrys like a clean tablecloth, and pink blooms dressed the wild scrub apples the color of a blushing bride. The large open fields were no longer being worked. However, you could still see divisions where sunny hayfields had produced bales, fertile plowed earth had yielded corn, and cows had pastured and laid down to chew their cud in the grass.

I slowly walked out further into the field, lost in thought, as I distanced myself further and further from my home. Soft feathery seed heads of timothy grass tickled my hand as I ran it over their fuzzy, seeded tops. Every so often, I would see the bubble-like home of a small spittle-bug glistening on the stem of the tall green grass. An orange and black butterfly skipped from yellow buttercup to yellow buttercup near me, and I watched its journey as it lit briefly to taste the flower's sweetness, then travel onward. There were no close neighbors near us on this hill. Only the tall, two-story, slate gray farmhouse further down the road that belonged to my mother-in-law. I looked wistfully that way and wished it had been different.

I had met Samuel one summer while visiting my married older sister. Although Samuel and I lived almost sixty miles apart and a river separated us, we became best friends and sweethearts early in high school after that meeting. We married the year I was a school senior, and not long after that we started a family. We had built our home on a section of land parceled off from the family farm. In the beginning, living there seemed like such a good idea. Samuel had gotten the land in a settlement when he was eighteen. His father had left his family to live with another woman and he abandoned the dairy farm, his two children, and Samuel's mother. Samuel was deeded half the farm by his guilty father in the divorce agreement. His father deserved to feel guilty because he was heaping so much onto Samuel's young shoulders. From that time on, Samuel had to do all the heavy work of the farm by himself with just a little help from the others.

After his father left, Samuel held down a part-time job to make ends meet, worked the farm, and at the same time tried to console his distraught mother. By that time, his father had moved several states away. Samuel's father did not help him or give advice or even stay in touch. It was like he had just been a few chapters in Samuel's life and now he had closed that book and was moving on to author another story and end the one he had been living. Just a couple of years later, Samuel's mother said, "Samuel, I need to get your name off the deed as being co-owner of the farm. You aren't twenty-one yet and I want to take out a mortgage. The bank does not like you being underaged with your name on the deed." She promised half the farm would always be there when he wanted it. He trusted in his mother's word and signed all his rights back to her and only kept the seven acres for himself. That was where we had built our home. It was right down the road from that tall, old gray farmhouse where his mother still lived.

Some years passed and the dairy was gone. Samuel's mother sold off all the cows and farm machinery one day. Samuel now worked full time as a mechanic for a trucking company, and we had two young children, Grace and Lucas. Recently we had a feeling of panic when we got the shocking news that the shop where Samuel worked was cutting everyone's hours and even might be closing in the near future. A gas shortage was going on all over the United States. Television broadcasts showed angry, impatient drivers waiting in long lines at stations everywhere to get the scarce, high-priced gas. The economy screeched to an abrupt halt, and many businesses were closing. The recession hit the long and short-haul truckers harder than most groups. Besides the inflated cost and scarcity of diesel, truckers had little merchandise or supplies to move. Production of goods had fallen way off too. When the truckers were not making money hauling on the road, their trucks didn't need work done on them. Repair shops, such as the one Samuel worked at, were now going bankrupt and closing their doors for good.

Unemployment was way up, especially in the rural area where we lived. New homes were not being built, new cars were not selling, and people were extremely cautious about purchasing anything that was not absolutely necessary. There was an atmosphere of fear everywhere. Everyone wondered if we were going to have another depression like the one in 1929. Samuel and I also wondered how we could survive financially if his shop did close. It was hard to get a decent job in our rural area, and work that offered a real chance for advancement and benefits was even scarcer. Could he get another job right away if that happened? We didn't think so. How could we survive without him working? We had never needed welfare and the thought of requiring help like that was frightening to us.

There was the option of Samuel joining the army. The Vietnam War was going on overseas. Even though we were winning the war, there was always a push for more men to join the fighting. More than 400,000 U.S. military men and women were fighting in that faraway jungle. If he signed up, he would have a secure job with regular pay and benefits. Samuel was young and healthy enough to be a soldier. However, neither of us wanted him to make the sacrifice of being away from his children. When his father left without warning, it struck Samuel awfully hard. My father had left my mother too. We did not want our children to be raised without a dad around for any reason. And the possibility of Samuel losing his life in combat was a risk we certainly did not want him to take. If there was a critical need for men to go to war, he probably would do that, but that was not the case right now. Many young men and women were gladly serving. I didn't know how military wives could spend their days raising their children alone. Military men and women gave up so much to serve, plus they put their lives in danger for all of us. Their spouses and children served our country too. I did not think I had the courage to sacrifice as they did.

Trying to make life-altering decisions about what we should do in the looming future was heaping more stress onto our already overburdened lives. Word came that the parent company approved of his work record and skills so much, they were offering him a transfer to a large truck shop in Hyattsville, Maryland. They asked Samuel if wanted to take that position and transfer there if the shop had to close down.

The thought of moving several states away had never crossed our minds. Now, it was an option we needed to consider. He was one of the few lucky ones in his shop offered a transfer. There wasn't much chance of him finding other work near our home, so it was a blessing in more ways than one that we could seriously think of moving away.

We had both been raised in small, country towns. We had gone to school with the same neighbors year after year and had never even spent time visiting a big city. If we moved, we would experience a different side of life, a side that sounded more exciting than living on a dirt road where little change happened day to day. If Lester's favorite cow had twin calves, it was big news around here. Even the town's snowplow accidentally knocking over the math teacher's mailbox was news in our small local newspaper.

A move like that would mean a more challenging job for Samuel plus the perk of a higher hourly wage. There would be more money to pay bills and get things for our children. We might even be able to put money away for the future. That would be a change. Samuel would also receive additional training to improve his mechanical skills. He would become a more valuable employee that a company would want to keep. Things were only getting worse, staying on this hill. It was an offer we really needed to consider.

I worked as a graphic artist at a small printing company, but my job wasn't going anywhere. Weeks earlier, I had gone to my boss with a concern. He had hired a new employee who was getting paid twice as much per hour than I, and the new man didn't have half the skills I did. Why didn't they value me as much as him, I wondered. Besides, it was just so unfair—I deserved a good wage like that too. I worked up enough courage to talk to my boss. He was sitting at his desk reading something when I knocked on his half-open office door. "Come on in," he said, and motioned me inside.

After exchanging the usual, "Hello, how are you doing today?" I cleared my throat and told him, "I'd like to talk to you about something that's bothering me."

He put the papers he was reading down, leaned back in his chair, and asked, "Well, what can I help you with? Take a seat and we'll talk about it."

He motioned to the chair next to his desk and I sat down, nervously shifted my weight, and tugged at my skirt's hem to be sure it was straight and covered my knees. Then I spoke. "The new man you hired seems friendly. He's learning fast and doing good work."

"Oh, I'm glad to hear everyone is getting along."

I hesitated, took a deep breath, and told him calmly, "Well, I found out by chance that you're paying him twice as much as me." I paused and scanned his face to see if he was getting upset, then continued. "I don't think that's fair since I have much more experience than he does, and I do typesetting for you besides the graphic artwork." I swallowed hard and tried to maintain an attitude of confidence as I anxiously waited for his reply.

"I see . . ." he said raising his eyebrows. "How did you find this out?"

"He volunteered the information. He was bragging about making so much more money than he did on his last job."

My boss slowly shook his head. "Well, he shouldn't have done that. I'll have to remind him to be quiet about his hourly wage. That information should be kept as confidential business between him and me. Is that all?"

I was baffled for a moment. Then I realized my boss was not understanding the reason for my visit or perhaps he was avoiding it. I plunged forward. "I would like to make as much as he does since we do the same work—well, actually, I do more than he does."

An uneasy silence hung in the air as moments passed and I awaited his response. Then he asked me, "Josey, you have worked for us for a few years now. Didn't we hold your job for you when you had your last child? If I remember correctly, you were out for, what, four or five weeks that time? We had to hire a temp to cover for you."

"Yes, you did let me come back to work after that, and I appreciate it. This is different though. I have more job duties, and he's starting at a much higher wage. I could use that extra money."

"Doesn't your husband have a good job, Josey?"

"Yes, but what does that have to do with it? I have to work as well."

"Your husband is the head of the family and the main wage earner. Anything you earn is extra money. The new guy is the head of his family. He should be paid more than someone like you who has another income. That's how it works. A man should make more than his wife." He stared straight at me, firm in his reasoning, then, perhaps seeing my shoulders slump, he added, "I probably could give you a little more per hour. How about fifteen cents more? That amounts to six dollars a week, more if you're doing overtime. Plus, you know you get a raise once a year already. That should make you happy," he said. Satisfied he had resolved the issue, he picked up the papers he had been reading and said it was nice talking to me.

I was dismissed and disappointed but didn't want to anger my boss by being too assertive. I could lose my job altogether. He believed men worked for the bills and women worked for play money or the "frills." It was useless to argue with that old-fashioned mentality. It would cause friction that could come back to hurt me. I didn't press my boss any further, even though I still felt it was unfair. The offer of Samuel's job relocation came at a perfect time. I might be able to get a higher-paying job away from my current employment and my boss's reasoning.

Samuel's shop began working only part-time for several weeks as they had warned us. Then the decision was made to shut the truck repair shop down completely after there was nothing for the men to do. With all the previous weeks of his shortened work hours, we had fallen behind in our mortgage and we were late paying other bills as well. Our credit was damaged, so we borrowed from one of those quickie finance companies that loan money to anyone so we could consolidate and pay bills. But the interest rate was terrible. If we were late just a few days, a huge late fee was added to our payment. It became even harder to pay what was due the next time. Similar to a snowball rolling downhill, our debt kept rolling out of control, growing too large to stop, and now our income to pay any of it off was threatened.

As I walked along, my foot struck a small brown nest on the ground. Curious, I bent over and picked up the tight, baseball-size round made of packed, dried grasses. When I pulled it apart to see the inside, it was warm and dry. It was most likely the abandoned home of a pretty deer mouse. They have a white bib, small pink, rounded ears, shiny black eyes, and soft camel-colored fur. I pictured the cute little mouse curled up in the sheltered hollow of this nest, snuggled deep into the soft dry covers of fine grass, as it dreamed away the long, cold winter.

I had caught one in a trap under the sink in the kitchen before. I hated killing those mice. Regular gray house mice didn't bother me as much to find in a trap, but deer mice, they were special. They were an animal of the field and wildflowers. Deer mice preferred living in the timothy grass, with the daisies blooming over their heads and tunnels of sweet pink clover to run through. They munched on the seeds of birdsfoot trefoil, sweet strawberries, grasses, and mushrooms that grew in their wild green home. I wished it had never come into my home where it had ended that idealistic life.

I stood lost in thought, holding the small empty nest in my hands. A black and white Bobolink flew past and then perched on a weathered gray fence post that held up the rusty length of barbed wire. He was not a pretty bird. He had a splash of yellow on him, but his black body with white markings on his back reminded me of a skunk. It was his song, oh, his song, which was so amazing. He puffed up his feathers, opened his beak wide, and sang out all the joy in his heart with an extended tumble of jazzy birdsong notes. What joy there was in his melody. Joy for the beauty of the day and sunshine on his wings and the fields. Joy for his freedom to go where he wanted, when he wanted. His song was earnestly jubilant as he claimed this patch of the timothy field as his own and celebrated this glorious summer day. I looked again at the tall, imposing farmhouse down the road. The Bobolink knew exactly where he should be. I was still uncertain if I was welcome at this place.

I drew in a deep breath and let it out slowly. The smell of the fresh, clean air filled my lungs and gave me clarity. I dropped the nest where I had found it and headed home. Samuel had wanted to know what I thought of taking that job and moving away. I had made a decision. Yes, I should tell Samuel we needed a change, and the job in Maryland offered stability, higher pay for him, and help to get us out of our financial predicament. Hopefully, I could also find a better job for me.

Our children were quite young, so we didn't have to worry about taking them out of school. I could probably find a babysitter to watch them down there. That was a scary thought. You never knew if you could trust a stranger with your children. There were so many news stories about babysitters slapping or abusing the children they took care of. Now, a cousin I trusted, with children of her own, babysat ours while Samuel and I worked. I did not want someone strange taking care of our children. But I might be forced to do that.

Hyattsville, Maryland, the new job location, was right next to Washington, DC, and Samuel and I had talked about what benefits there might be living near that big city. It would be a chance to see exciting things such as the Smithsonian Museum. We could visit the National Zoo, the Lincoln Memorial, and maybe even the White House. Those places we had only seen in pictures and never thought we could visit. We might also become "sophisticated," I had joked, and we laughed at that word. Samuel's mother had a saying, "You can't catch what you are not exposed to." And we certainly weren't exposed to much culture where we were now. We would always be "rednecks," but adding a little culture and sophistication to our lives wouldn't hurt our children or us one bit. It all sounded so exciting and interesting and so much like a fun adventure.

I would tell Samuel we should move away from the home we had lived in since we married. We should try for a better life in Hyattsville. I still wasn't absolutely sure it was the right choice, but that was the decision I had come to and would talk to him about. I crossed the field and headed back home. I hoped he would agree and that it would not be a serious mistake. Only time would tell.

## Chapter 2

Samuel and I had a long, serious talk later. After going over all the pros and cons, he agreed that we needed to move. We would sink further into debt if we stayed and tried to live on my pay plus his unemployment. The prospects of him finding another job locally were so hopeless. We would rent our home on a year's lease just in case we had to move back. The new job in Maryland might not be as great as it sounded. We might also get homesick.

We took a quick trip to DC to check out rental properties close to his new work on Kenilworth Avenue. It was shocking to find out how much rent they wanted for decent apartments. We needed so much money for the apartment's first and last month's rent, the security deposit, fees for hooking up utilities, plus what it would cost to move our things. It was also surprising that many areas near his work were predominately all-black developments or all-white areas. The Fair Housing Act had been passed and signed by President Lyndon Johnson to forbid discrimination in housing due to race or color, but it didn't appear that much had changed in Maryland or Washington. It was still mostly divided into neighborhoods with predominately one race or another. I wondered, were they staying segregated in some areas by choice?

I was looking forward to living in a place that included people of other cultures. We had no diversity in the small country school I had attended. Everybody looked pretty much the same as their neighbor in our town. We weren't taught much about the heritage or culture of southern people or people with different backgrounds than us. The total sum of my social education regarding people of color had been that George Washington Carver gave us peanuts. I had learned little to nothing about the lives of other races and did not understand why anyone would be thought of as less or enslaved because their skin was different.

I was a young girl in the 1950s when I saw a black family for the first time. Karl had been stationed on the USS *Leary* and his ship was due to come into port at Norfolk, Virginia. He had been out to sea when a serious fire happened onboard, so the destroyer was returning to Norfolk for major repairs. My parents missed him a great deal and were genuinely concerned, but it would be a short shore leave, so we drove down from central New York to greet the ship when it came in. We took a ferry while there to reach the Norfolk navy base. It was so exciting to ride on that strange boat that carried cars, and people too. I was about ten years old and had never been far from the dirt road farm where I grew up. It was all such an exciting new adventure.

I walked to the boat's railing and peered over it at the dark, foamy water the propeller was stirring up. Far off in the distance, I could see the land where we were heading. Looking around the deck, I noticed signs on the bathroom doors and above the drinking fountain that stated in bold letters, "FOR WHITES ONLY." My eyes went from those signs to those of a little black girl about my age standing with her family. Her mother was sheltering her tight against her legs like a mother hen would shelter a chick. I thought about those signs. Then, I walked over to my mother and asked loudly, "Mommy, where do the black people go to the bathroom?" Several heads turned our way when people heard my question. My mother, embarrassed and unsure of this different environment, told me to shush. She took my hand and led me back to the railing, away from the others. Then she bent down to my level and quietly told me, "They can't go to the bathroom here. They have to wait."

"But Mom, what if they're thirsty? The sign on the drinking fountain says, 'WHITES ONLY' too. Why can't the black people have a drink?" I asked, "Why?"

Looking around and uneasy, she put her finger on my lips as a sign to be quiet. A heavy man with his back to the railing was mouthing a fat, smelly cigar. He gazed steadily at us as he listened to everything we said. She told me quietly but firmly again, "They have to wait, they have to hold it, now stop asking questions. That's just the way it is." I did stop asking questions, but I never understood why those signs were there. Now, years later, I was married and relocating to Maryland close to that same area with my family, and that question had never been answered.

* * *

Samuel and I continued our search. Our apartment needed to be near an elementary school somewhere around Hyattsville, Maryland. A qualified school was important since our daughter was almost ready for kindergarten. We had to keep that in mind as we checked out the offerings. Most of the places for rent in our price range looked shabby or uncared for by management or were in rundown neighborhoods. The local elementary school looked neglected and unsuitable as well.

After crossing off several listings, we checked an apartment close to Samuel's work. It was a few miles across the Washington, DC, border in Bladensburg, Maryland. The new complex consisted of three-story modern brick buildings with lots of windows, balconies, and pristine landscaping. As we walked to the office, a holly tree with red berries caught my eyes. That was something I had only seen on Christmas cards. Everything looked green and well-maintained.

A friendly, petite rental agent interviewed us and answered our questions. She looked like a model from a magazine advertising the latest fashionable attire for work and had a stylish hairdo and perfectly manicured fingernails. More than one diamond ring on her finger flashed as she pointed out some features of the complex in a printed brochure. It looked like she had diamond stud earrings on as well. *What a fantastic job she must have to afford all that bling,* I thought. We talked briefly and then she took us to see a garden apartment on the ground floor.

"You folks are incredibly lucky this apartment is still available. Almost all our units are already rented," she told us. We followed her down the sidewalk, through an outside door, and into a hallway. She fiddled with a bunch of jingling keys, unlocked a heavy gray metal door, and pushed it open.

"You have a solid door here with three locks," she proudly pointed out. "There's a lock on the handle, an additional deadbolt lock, and a chain lock."

"Three locks?" I asked her. "We never even locked one door at our house."

"Really?" she replied, raising her eyebrows and looking puzzled. "It is safe here, but you'll want to lock your doors, just to be secure. Look, it even has a peephole to check out who's in the hall before you open it."

I put my eye close to the peephole and looked out. It was impossible to see much hallway through such a small opening.

She kept up her sales talk and added, "And we plan to get surveillance cameras soon for all the entrances."

Alarmed, I asked about the need for all that security. "Is this a high crime area?"

She waved her hand. "Oh no, that's standard for modern apartments these days," she told me, dismissing my concern. We stepped into the bright living/dining area.

"This open concept is all new," she said as she showed us the spacious empty room that was open to the kitchen and dining area while sweeping her hand like a model on television showing merchandise.

The apartment smelled and looked brand new and clean. The empty walls were painted a warm, light cream color. There was no carpet, just tile, but there was a new set of drapes on the glass doors. She pointed out more features of the living room, dining room, and kitchen area.

"You have built-in fire alarms, and see those shiny little disks above? Those are your sprinklers," she said, pointing to the ceiling. "You have a lot of choices here with how you can decorate and arrange your furniture.

You can put a nice area rug down and place your sofa and chairs several different ways."

I was thinking about the lack of furniture we had now. I could never fill the rooms with the little we had kept. She walked over and opened the drapes on the glass doors to show us the view.

"These white drapes come with the apartment and must stay on the glass doors. Please do not change them. We like to have all the units look the same when you see the outside of the complex. It makes for more continuity in the appearance of our apartments."

She kept speaking. "You have an excellent view of our fantastic pool from here, and this is your security locking bar for this door." She pushed on a long metal bar that spanned the glass door. It folded upwards in half, and she slid the door open. "By the way, we have a paid lifeguard here too. He's quite handsome also," she said, winking at me. "This is your own concrete patio for relaxing in lounge chairs." She smiled and added, "You can have flower boxes out here and even garden if you want."

I thought of the big garden I grew at home with peas, beans, carrots, potatoes, tomatoes, squash, and corn and laughed to myself about trying to fit all that into a couple of flower boxes. I whispered to Samuel as she slid the door closed and locked it. "She has no idea what a real garden is." However, the clear, sparkling water in the blue pool did look inviting. There was a children's wading area on one end and a deeper diving area on the other. *That pool will be fun for all of us,* I thought.

I remembered when Samuel and I had a date at the local swimming hole on Choconut Creek back home. The water slowed down around a bend in the stream, and a deep basin pool formed there surrounded by tree-lined banks. A thick, knotted rope hung from a limb on an old leaning willow. It was a great rope to swing on, then drop down into the water. This fancy sparkling pool at the complex had no rope swing and wasn't private but looked even more inviting. I was glad it would be our view out the glass door and not a parking lot full of cars. I wanted to avoid staring out my windows at the shiny metal grills of autos.

Next, the agent led us to the kitchen and pointed out all the new appliances. The kitchen was perfect. It was the right size, and it came with a dishwasher. What a tremendous help that would be.

"Lots of room here for storage also, no wasted space," she said as she demonstrated the Lazy Susan cupboard in the corner. I really liked that cupboard.

She led us down the hallway and pointed out the roomy bathroom. The two bedrooms back there had sunlight streaming into the rooms through large windows. We were impressed. The apartment was roomy enough, fresh, clean, and hit all the points we wanted, plus more. It was close to Samuel's work and near a suitable elementary school.

"You also have built-in air conditioning. It gets hot down here in the south, you know, extremely hot and humid." That would be a substantial change from home, where I just opened screened windows when it got hot, and that was enough. Then she asked us, "So, is this going to be your new home?" When we didn't answer immediately, she added, "I should also tell you, we are very, very careful what kind of people we rent our apartments to. We don't let any undesirable types qualify to rent here, if you know what I mean. I'm sure you folks from the north will be comfortable here."

Samuel and I gave each other a questioning look and nodded our heads at the same time. Then he reached out, shook her hand, and said, "We'll take it."

"Great!" she said, smiling wide. "Let's go back to my office and get all the paperwork filled out. I'll take your deposit, and you can move right in when you're ready."

Samuel and I sold everything that wasn't an absolute necessity to get enough money to rent a truck, cover travel costs, and make all the necessary down payments. All we kept was our clothing, some kitchen items, and beds and dressers for our family. We would have to buy more furniture later. Right now, we needed the funds more, and with the little we were taking, Samuel could pack everything into a small U-Haul trailer to tow behind our car.

I never dreamed I would live in a place with a built-in pool. The kids and I would have so much fun swimming there. The rent was over our budget, which meant we would be strapped for money each month, but I would get a job right away. With Samuel's higher pay from his new job, plus mine, we hoped it would be doable.

* * *

Finding work for me was quite challenging. Washington, DC, had many areas I would be insecure working in. I read the help-wanted advertisements in the *Washington Post* and studied maps but didn't know what kind of neighborhood the business advertising for help was in. I didn't know anything about the businesses' reputations either. They could treat their employees terrible and could be constantly rehiring. The city and its suburbs were so big, it was frustrating to figure out where I should be looking. Finally, feeling hampered by my lack of knowledge, I contacted an employment agency.

The Spring Street Agency advertised they found the best employment for qualified workers, and when I spoke with a representative, he told me they had lots of postings near where we lived for people with my skills. Payments on the $300 fee they charged would be due monthly. And I did not have to make the first payment until I had been on my new job for thirty days. They assured me it would be an excellent job, including benefits with a good company, and well worth their high fee.

The first placement they offered me was working at a large photo lab. It was a company with government contracts from all branches of the military. It sounded like an easy job. My duties would be reviewing aerial and other photographs, processing and duplicating them, and filing them away.

They wanted someone capable of working independently and with an "artistic eye" to adjust the color and crop or focus on certain portions of the photos if needed. The pay was much more than I had been getting up north. It included several paid holidays, health insurance, bonuses. It sounded great—almost too good to be true. Then the employment agent told me there was one downside to it. Some photos were quite graphic. The Vietnam War was going on, and there were lots of casualty photos of both sides of the conflict. I thought of going to work every day and studying pictures of wounded or dead men, women, and children. No high hourly wage or benefits could make that job attractive to me. I quickly turned that one down.

The next job they offered sounded awesome. It was for a paste-up artist at AdArt&Tech, an advertising agency in DC. I had a tough time believing they would even consider me for a job like that. I told him, "No, I'm not good enough to work in a place like that. I never went to college." But the agent encouraged me to go to the interview anyway. The advertising agency would like someone with an advanced degree but would consider an applicant with on-the-job training. He said that even if I didn't get hired, it would be a good practical experience to go for the job interview and get comfortable doing them. Reluctantly, I agreed, and he set a date for me to meet with the company representative. I searched through my art portfolio and carefully pulled out anything that looked amateurish. It would be better to show them a few well-designed pieces than a bunch of mediocre art. I had samples of letterheads and business cards I had designed for several companies and brochures and logos I had created. I included a few newsletters for corporations and service groups I had worked on, all complete with photos included in the printed artwork. I was proud of what I had done and hoped it would be enough to impress them. I braced myself, though, because I was sure they would never hire me.

On the day of the interview, I summoned up my courage and put on a slate gray skirt and crisp white blouse. It was my most professional-looking outfit. Because I was so unfamiliar with the area and driving in DC, Samuel volunteered to drive me. I had always hoped to move up the ladder on the job in my art career. This would be a wonderful job if I were hired. However, I was absolutely sure my skills and experience would not be enough for what they would expect. The job description was not for an artist to do creative design work. But I could always hope that when they saw my artistic ability, they would assign more creative work in the future. That is, on the extremely remote chance they *did* hire me.

Samuel kissed me, told me to be calm and confident, not scared, and wished me good luck when he dropped me off. He would find a parking space nearby and wait for me. My heart raced as I entered AdArt&Tech and asked for the art director. The friendly receptionist led me to a conference room and gave me a handful of papers to fill out. There were pages of questions about my work experience and personal data. It was annoying to write down all that information again because it was already on my résumé along with the papers Spring Street Agency had forwarded to them. I finished filling the pages out and looked around the room as

I waited. The walls held several awards for advertising excellence. There were logos of well-known companies and even local news stations that used their services. Looking closer, I saw a picture of someone shaking President Kennedy's hand and another one of a man with President Johnson.

*This place is never going to hire me,* I said to myself after seeing all those awards and photos. I sat there nervously for several minutes, believing I should run out the door rather than face the humiliation of rejection. But before I could bolt, two men wearing white shirts, dark slacks, and expensive ties entered the room and shook my hand. Ted Wickham introduced himself as the art director. He told me the man with him was the layout department's manager, Dean. Ted led the questions as he looked over the pages of my written application. Dean opened my portfolio and started leafing through it. He looked up at me once in a while as he listened to my answers to Ted's questions and explanations.

Ted described what my job duties would be. "We need a paste-up and layout artist who can combine type with photographs and illustrations for publications and other artwork. You'll need to create pages for brochures, advertisements, overhead projections, slides, and other graphic work and work independently. Occasionally, you may have to do a cover design or create a logo for a company, but the majority of it is putting pages together. Can you do all that?"

"Yes, I'm familiar with doing most of that," I told him.

"How long have you been doing paste-up?" Ted asked.

"For a couple of years now," I replied. "I was in charge of doing it at the print shop where I worked. I designed logos and brochures, plus we did any graphic artwork a business needed to be printed." I didn't tell them the print shop was part of a sheltered workshop for disabled people. I wasn't disabled, but they had hired me to do the pre-press work so the disabled employees could do commercial printing and other print shop jobs like collating, folding, and stapling. I didn't specify on my résumé that there was only one printing press there. We didn't even do four-color work. *Let them assume it was a bigger print shop,* I thought when I had put the résumé together. "Don't give too many details" was the advice I'd read about writing one. I didn't lie, I just left out some minor facts. I had written, "Responsible for all pre-press preparation and graphic design at a print shop. Created logos, brochures, posters, professional business stationery, etc." All that was true.

I could not help but notice as I talked with Ted that he had a pronounced tick in his left eye. *Is working at this agency that stressful?* I wondered.

Ted was saying, "Sometimes we get a job with a tight deadline to meet, especially the government jobs, and we'll need you to work overtime. Can you stay late here in the city if we need you to do that?" he asked.

"Sure," I answered, "I can do that." Silently, I wondered how I would manage that with the kids. I'd deal with that problem later. I wondered what kind of government jobs they did. I hoped it was nothing like the military photo lab work I had turned down.

Ted cleared his throat, stared straight at me, and asked, "And are you pregnant or planning on getting pregnant in the near future?"

I had heard that question before. Many times, it was printed right on the job applications. Most places never paid for the time a woman had to take off to give birth. Instead, they resented the interruption of a woman missing work to have a child and upsetting their business schedules. Quite often, when a new mother called her workplace to say the doctor had approved her return, she found out she had been permanently replaced and no longer had a job.

"No," I answered, "we don't plan on any more children right away." There was a good chance I might get pregnant, though, in the future. I was allergic to those new birth control pills that you took every day. *God, I hope they can't see I'm stretching the truth in more ways than one,* I thought as I shifted my weight in the chair, desperate to project a confident demeanor.

"And I see you can type too. That's a real bonus. You'll need to do that here to set headlines and photo captions."

"Yes, I can type. Not fast, but accurate," I answered.

"Accurate is a necessity here. It costs hundreds of dollars to trash a publication or promo that has a serious typo in it. Yes, we certainly prefer accuracy over speed." Ted was quiet for a moment, then continued. "Well, we're strapped for help. Your art skills and your typing skills are a real asset.

A lot of artists aren't typists, and you're both. Work is backing up, and we're falling behind on meeting important deadlines. Our clients don't like that and are complaining. So far, you're the best candidate they've sent us," Ted said. He turned and asked Dean, "What do you think?"

"I like what I see here," Dean said, patting my portfolio after he closed it.

Ted looked down at the floor like he was studying his shoe tips. He let out a long audible sigh, then stood and told Dean, "Let's step outside for a minute." They left the room, and I could hear their muffled voices on the other side of the door. I strained to make out the words but couldn't. I was sure that at any minute they would reenter and say thank you, but no thank you. Instead, Ted Wickham reopened the door and said, "Congratulations, can you start next week?"

Too quickly, I rose and blurted out, "Yes, I can do that." In my mind, I was trying to figure out who would babysit the children. I grinned from ear to ear, shook their hands, and gushed, "Thank you, oh, thank you both. I'll be here in a week ready to work. I'm looking forward to it." I said goodbye and rushed past them to leave before they could change their minds.

I left the agency and hardly felt the city sidewalk I was walking on. I could not believe my luck. I kissed Samuel hard as soon as I got into the car and said, "I got the job!"

"I'm so happy for you." He kissed me again, only much more deeply this time.

"Whoa, fella," I said, "we've got a whole day ahead of us yet, and you've got to get to work. Your boss only gave you two hours off. We'll celebrate later after the kids go to bed."

"All right," Samuel replied, rubbing my thigh. He grinned at me as he turned the key in the ignition. "But I'll be thinking of you all day, and it's going to be one hell of a celebration."

"Sounds good to me," I said, smiling like a kid anticipating a special present.

It was incredible. I was going to work in a prestigious advertising agency in Washington, DC! My dream job was coming true. They even offered me more per hour than I had been getting up north, where, if I got a twenty-cent raise a year, I felt lucky. I hadn't attended college for my art career. I'd gotten pregnant soon after we married, just out of high school. I thought of each job I'd taken as furthering my education and a chance to learn and advance my skills. My first job was at a small sign shop doing menial work, like painting wooden sign blanks and answering the phone. Later, I worked in a large sign shop and learned about different fonts and how to letter signs and do silk screening. The last job I had before Samuel's transfer was at that small print shop for disabled people, where I was part of the staff doing artwork and design for publications.

Traveling back to our new apartment, I was so excited, I kept chatting away nonstop, telling Samuel about the agency and the awards and pictures of the presidents and major businesses I had seen hanging on the wall. I told him about the men I had talked to and my high hopes for this job. Then I began having second thoughts. Could I do the work they needed of me at the agency? Would I make a lot of mistakes because I knew so little about what people actually did at an advertising agency? Would I get fired right away? Elation gave way to nervous anxiety, even fear of what might happen.

We needed to figure out the childcare problem now and how to make that work. I didn't want to leave the children with anyone we didn't know, and everyone around us was a stranger. We had seen more than one news story of babysitters neglecting children in some way, even slapping them when the parents weren't there. How could we protect our children from that happening to them?

Samuel and I talked more about it, and I asked him, "Do you think it's possible for you to work the second shift so you could watch the kids while I worked during the daytime? Then when I come home, we could have supper together and after you could go to work. We would keep the kids safe at our apartment and save on childcare expenses. Do you think that would be okay? Could we do that?"

"You mean you want me to babysit the kids?" he asked.

"No, silly, not babysit. You're their dad—you would be taking care of them like I do, not babysitting."

He paused, considering the idea. "I think I could, and yes, it would be the best thing for the kids. I'll give it a try if my boss goes along with changing my hours."

Samuel's boss was happy to have him work the second shift. That even meant slightly more pay. The need for a babysitter was solved. Life was looking better for us already. The children would be safe with their father watching them. We would have enough income from my work as well to pay the monthly rent and start replacing some furniture we had sold. I was going to work in an advertising agency! Wow, what a big step up the ladder for me. Going to sleep was hard for a few nights. I kept thinking about my new job and how well things were working out for us both in Bladensburg.

I missed my country home, but this big city and the opportunities happening for us were so exciting. Samuel and I had needed this time to ourselves. I had not known my mother-in-law well when we got married. I should have gotten to know her better. Maybe then I might have foreseen some of the problems. It wasn't long after our marriage that troubles started to happen.

I loved my mother-in-law, but even though Samuel had married and left home, she still wanted to control his life. That included his wife and children, too. Daily prying reports were required from Samuel in person or by phone. We both thought his mother had too much free time on her hands. We urged her to get a job, volunteer, start a hobby, or do something else to occupy herself and give us some privacy, but there was no observing boundaries with her. I knew I was quite different from my mother-in-law. Men don't usually marry someone like their mother. Instead, they often marry someone completely opposite of their mother. Such diverse types of women in close interactions can sometimes cause tension. I was a shy, private person; my mother-in-law was not. We were different in so many other ways.

Samuel hinted politely to please let us have more time by ourselves, but each day, the phone would ring just minutes after Samuel arrived home. He would have to tell her everything about his workday and anything else she grilled him about. I wondered how she got the timing so perfect. One day, just before Samuel got home, I saw a lace curtain pulled back from the window down the road at the gray farmhouse. A figure was standing there watching the road. I realized she was watching for Samuel to come home. When the phone rang each day, I would keep busy getting supper ready while Samuel answered question after question from his mother. I told the kids to play or watch TV while they waited for Daddy to talk to them.

One time, I heard a scrap of Samuel's conversation with her. He was saying, "Yes, she does do that. No, Mother, she does not. Now, why would you ask a thing like that?" I realized she was grilling him about more than just his work. By the time Samuel could finally hang up after giving the detailed daily report and I asked, "So, how was your day dear?" he was pretty much talked out. He didn't want to go over it all again. One time, Samuel suggested to his mother to wait until after our supper, and he would call her later in the evening to talk. He also tried asking his mother not to call every day—they could touch base every few days instead. That didn't work for her either. She didn't want to accept any boundaries or give up control of him. It was as if he was still stepping off the school bus.

Recently, I had a conversation with a close neighbor. It was unsettling to find out what my mother-in-law was saying.

"This is a little awkward, and I don't know how to say this gently, Josey," she said. "But your mother-in-law told me you're neglecting her son and your children."

"What?" I asked. "Neglecting them, how? What does she mean?"

"She said you shouldn't be working. You should be home where you belong, taking care of your own children and not having someone else raise your kids. She also said you should stay home to support your husband and be there when he needs you."

"Wow . . ." I shook my head and let out a long sigh. Then I asked, "But doesn't she understand that I'm taking care of my children's needs and supporting my husband by earning the extra we need to survive?"

My friend answered, "No, I really don't think so, Josey. She says you're being selfish and only want a career of your own."

"This is too much. What do I have to do to make her happy with me?"

"I don't know," my friend replied. "But I'm not the only neighbor she mentioned that to."

This move to Hyattsville, Maryland, was going to be a blessing in more ways than one.

## Chapter 3

I left early the following week to make sure I arrived on time for my first day of work. Samuel had done most of the driving around town since we moved to Bladensburg. I was still insecure about driving the busy and confusing streets in such a large city as Washington, DC, but he would be watching the children, so I had to do it now. There was a tricky place going around Logan Circle that always caused traffic to slow to a crawl and back up. I soon learned that foreign diplomats double parked all day long in that area and blocked the flow of traffic with their large Chryslers, Mercedes, Rolls-Royces, and Lincoln Continentals. It was so difficult and annoying to have those limos sticking way out in traffic. Trying to thread my way around them slowed me down so much that I feared I would be late arriving for my first day. Those diplomats didn't care about local laws. They had immunity from traffic tickets and other regulations that the rest of us had to abide by. When their chauffeurs got a ticket on their windshield, they simply laughed and tossed them like confetti.

Fortunately, I reached the parking lot next to the agency just in time and found a space. I quickly checked my hair in the rearview mirror, took a deep breath, and told myself firmly, "You can do this!" as I gathered my belongings. My new black briefcase held my Rapidograph technical pens, an Xacto knife, various triangles and templates, plus a special stainless-steel ruler with typesetting picas and line leading marks. Those were important tools often borrowed by coworkers and somehow disappeared on the job. I had been sure to tape my name on each one of them.

I was anxious. I didn't know what would be expected of me or what my coworkers would be like. I locked the car door, and as I walked past the other parked cars in the lot, I saw a sporty red car with a noticeable decal of the rebel flag on it. Right next to that was a yellow one with the words "Don't Tread On Me" and the image of a coiled rattlesnake. "Yup, I'm in the south now," I said to myself. I reached the entrance of the three-story modern building wedged in among other upscale office buildings on the block. The double glass door had large gold, modern lettering that spelled out AdArt&Tech Creative Group. I pushed it open and stepped inside the lobby.

The receptionist greeted me right away with a friendly, "Good morning, how can I help you?" There was a definite southern twang in her voice. I told her I was just hired and was reporting for a job in the layout department. She replied, "Oh, yes, I remember you now. You were here last week. Glad to see you back. Well, welcome to AdArt&Tech Creative Group. Y'all follow me, please." She led me to an elevator to the second floor. I wanted to tell her I had only ridden on an elevator two other times but didn't. She didn't need to know how inexperienced I was. Both times were in the hospital when my children were born. I nervously clutched my briefcase and adjusted the shoulder strap of my purse as the elevator rose.

"Are you temp or perm?" the receptionist asked.

My mind was wandering. It took me a few seconds to understand what she was asking. "Oh, I'm permanent, or at least I hope I am. We'll see."

"Oh, don't be so nervous," she said, waving her hand. "I'm sure y'all will do fine." Then she corrected herself and said, "That is, you will do fine. I'm sorry I keep slipping back into my southern drawl." I was about to ask where she was from when the elevator door opened to a busy scene, and I recognized Ted Wickham, the art director. He walked briskly by with a bunch of papers in his hands.

Ted stopped when he saw me and said, "Hello, Josey, so glad you're here. We really need you today." He still had that nervous twitch in his left eye when he spoke to me, and again, I wondered why.

Ted told the receptionist to show me where the layout department was and get Dean to help me. Dean was much more relaxed and friendly than when I had seen him in my interview, and he led me to the back area of the small layout department and pointed to an empty drafting table. "This will be your work desk, Josey," he told me, gesturing toward the large maple drafting table with a gliding silver straight edge on top. "I'll give you a few minutes to get settled in and be right back. I have to check on some art in the technical department. Oh, yes, welcome to the agency. Busy, busy place today. It's a Monday for sure," he said as he left the room.

I started to unpack my things and look around. Only four people were working in the department. Dean, the head of this area, had another drafting table up front by the door. A tall black coworker named Booker sat at another drafting table across from Dean's. Maria and Lyla, whom Booker introduced me to, were tucked into an alcove area to one side in the back of the room. They were typesetters and sat side by side with their desks touching. I was grateful my drafting table was alone in the back corner of the room. It was a perfect place to work privately. And back there, no one could watch me making the mistakes I was sure would come.

I could see how my coworkers did their jobs from that location too. It was the best situation for me to pull this off and blend in as if I knew what I was doing. I took my pens, Xacto knife, and ruler out of my briefcase, set them on my desk, and waited to see what Dean would ask me to do. Before long, Dean returned, asked me how I was doing, and then gave me an assignment.

It was an easy one-page paste-up with a photo and heading plus text. *I can handle this*, I thought, and focused on completing it. I carefully measured and drew the margins of the page on my paper with a special light blue pencil. It was a color the camera wouldn't pick up. I trimmed the galleys and the photo to size and figured out where the photo would fit within the copy. I couldn't break the copy where just part of a sentence would be left hanging by itself at the top of the page. That was called a "widow" and wasn't a good thing to have on a publication.

I had done this same procedure many times on my previous job, but nervousness about possibly doing it wrong in this environment made me work much slower and be more cautious. I waxed the back of the photo and type galley, then glued it all down, making sure the type wrapped around the photo attractively. Looking it all over, I was pleased with the result. The heading was centered, and the blocks of typesetting and photo fit together nicely. It was clean, with no smudges or marks that might be picked up by the camera.

When I was finished, Dean examined my work carefully and nodded his head in approval. He just reminded me to use registration marks at the top and bottom of each page I worked on (how had I forgotten them!), then he quickly brought me more to do. I was so busy and focused, the day passed by quickly. Soon I was on my way home. I was relieved I hadn't screwed something up. I had made it through my first day and was pleased I seemed to fit in.

* * *

The nervousness of that first day dissipated in the following weeks as I settled into work at the agency. I learned several new typesetting and graphic art skills. I used the headliner machine in a small room off the hallway. It produced long strips of larger-sized type on photographic paper. I sat at the keyboard and typed out headlines and photo captions in varied sizes. It was slow work. Each time I pushed a key, a flash of light exposed one character and then advanced the strip of paper to be ready for the next keystroke. When I was done, the machine forwarded the strips into a photographic chemical bath. Eventually, the type came out of the machine dry and in long strips, like a narrow photographic print about two inches wide and as long as needed. Those photo strips had to be cut apart, trimmed to size, and pasted down into galleys of type. I goofed a few times, putting some photo strips through the waxing machine the wrong side up. The hot adhesive beeswax, which acted like glue, came out on the front where the type was instead of the back where it was supposed to be. I quickly wiped the wax off the strips and ran them back through the correct way. I had only used a small hand-held waxer at my old job. You held it like an iron and ran it over the back of the strips to wax them. Here, the agency had a fancy desktop machine that you fed the galleys of type into, and you had to concentrate on sending them through face up or the wax would be on the wrong side.

I learned more about distinct types and names of fonts, point sizes (their height), and the leading used between lines of type. I also learned how to use kerning between characters, such as when an uppercase "A" fell beside a "V" to position them closer together. I focused on doing paste-ups of pages that were eye-catching, attractive, and, most import-ant of all, accurate and camera-ready. I prepared color separations by using my Xacto knife to cut thin Rubylith film for each color overlay and then registered the layers so they would print properly with each other layer. For publications, the pages had to be set up in signatures of several pages. That was a pressman's large sheet of paper with the pages positioned properly so they printed in chronological order and backed up correctly.

Those signatures would be printed, cut apart, folded, collated, and assembled into all sorts of publications such as brochures, manuals, re-ports, even books. The actual printing of all the publications was sourced out to print shops in the area. Everything needed to be prepared proper-ly. There was no pressman in the building to tell me I set something up wrong and he had caught it before it was printed. I would never talk to the pressman working in a printshop, producing publications from the agency, somewhere in Washington, Maryland, or Virginia.

As Ted Wickham had warned me, hundreds of dollars, possibly thou-sands of dollars, would be lost if an error had to be corrected and printed again. Reprints would be especially costly if they were four-color work, meaning they went through the presses four times. Once each for magen-ta red, cyan blue, lemon yellow, and finally for black ink. All the colors used in a publication came from a mixture of those four colors regardless of whether it was green or purple or any other.

I worked on brochures, learned how to make graphic art for slides and overheads, did business presentations, and prepped all types of print-ed materials. I was getting an education, adding to my skills, and getting paid at the same time. It was an on-the-job graphic art college and hard, demanding work with high-pressure deadlines. I loved it but was beginning to understand why Ted Wickham had that tick in his eye.

Occasionally, no matter how carefully I worked, I would misspell a word while creating the headlines. Our proofreader was good at catching typesetting mistakes for us. Priscilla was a young, attractive, single, well-spoken woman. She had graduated from William and Mary College and was responsible for proofing and editing everyone's work before the client finally approved it for printing. Priscilla gave off the aura of coming from wealth. I noticed she always wore expensive jewelry and clothing and probably did not need to work such a demanding job. I also wondered why she was there and especially why she would take on so much responsibility. She had to be sure spelling, punctuation, and content were accurate in those expensive publications. It wasn't a job I ever wanted to do. She didn't seem bothered by all that responsibility and took it in stride. Her persona didn't match that of my exacting high school English teacher, Mrs. Collins. She had dressed and acted like a sour prison matron when checking our English assignments.

One of my other coworkers in the layout department was Booker, the only black man I had seen at the agency. Booker left the room often. He was social and every day visited and chatted with coworkers from department to department. I wondered how he ever got his work done. Dean, my department head, was always working hard, reviewing pages we had put together or creating some sort of advertisement or fancy proposal to show a client. He was a family man and easy to get along with. He patiently showed me how to prepare finished artwork at the agency for a client to review.

First, a dark mat board backing was cut larger than the finished page of artwork, typesetting, and photos. Then a photograph of that finished paste-up was fastened to the center of the mat board, leaving a wide border all around. Next, a sheet of tracing paper was taped at the top edge to cover the photograph like it was something important that needed protecting. Finally, a cover of the finest quality light gray laid linen cardstock was taped onto the back and folded over to the front to make a flap-like book cover that protected the art and everything underneath.

The last item was to affix the AdArt&Tech logo with its gold lettering onto the bottom right corner of the cover. The customer had to lift the gray cover, then the tissue paper to reveal the photo of the artwork with its typesetting like the special present it was, precious and expensive. It was quite an impressive presentation when it was done just to show a customer one item.

Ted often came to Dean's desk to drop off new work or confer with him about a project. Dean would then hand the assignment to Booker or me or give it to the typesetters to work on. Everything that came in the door was always late getting to the agency, had a tight deadline to meet, and had to be completed as soon as possible. We did work for several DC, Maryland, and Virginia businesses, plus various branches of the United States government. Some of that work included reports for Senate or House committees and all the other government agencies, complete with graphs and charts and lots of boring statistics.

The technical department was in the room next door to layout and paste-up. There were only men working in that department. They did anything that required mechanical drafting, such as drawing diagrams, charts, graphs, and any other ink and line work. Those projects had to be done with black technical ink pens, triangles, compasses, and precise measurements on drafting satin, a kind of thick tracing paper. When they finished their work, copies were made in the photo department in the basement. The photos were then sent back up to us to be included in the publications we were working on.

Cade usually brought over copies of the technical drawings once they were sent back upstairs from the photo lab. He was a tall, slender man that seldom smiled and walked stiff-backed like a soldier reporting for duty. I noticed he would come into the room and walk right past Booker without saying anything. He would hand the drawings to Dean or me if Dean were out of the room. I almost expected he would salute at some point he was so stoic. He would never hand work to Booker and acted as if Booker wasn't even there. He seemed to always be uptight about something and not relaxed like Dean. He wasn't stressed in the same way Ted Wickham was, though. Ted had such a nervous tick that I was concerned for him. I didn't know what the major stress was in his life, but he wasn't coping well with it. Cade just always seemed to be pissed off.

The creative department artists were a completely different type from the rest of us. That's where I longed to work eventually. It was the department where you were handed an art assignment and told to design something special. Every kind of art supply was available to play with in there, and you could take whatever time you needed to come up with something impressive, within reason, of course. It was premium billing time the agency could charge a customer. Three artists worked in that room. It was all men as well. The radio blasted rock music when the owner or clients weren't around. It was an "off-limits" area for the rest of us. Those artists needed their space without interruptions that might impede their creative flow or whatever they did to earn the highest paychecks in the agency. Booker was in there once in a while, but the rest of us stayed out.

One of those artists, Jaimie, was a real bohemian type. He would show up in paint-spattered clothes and sandals that he would abandon to walk barefoot in the hallway while getting coffee and glazed donuts in the break room. He often wore a headband around his long, brown, unruly hair. His attire and demeanor were in sharp contrast to the rest of the male employees at the agency. The others wore white shirts and ties. Jaimie got away with wearing whatever he felt that day. Often it was a T-shirt and baggy olive-green kakis. It was humorous to see the receptionist rush down the hallway to the creative department to tell them to turn down the music because company was coming upstairs. Mr. Stevens, the AdArt&Tech owner, was entertaining a prospective client in the conference room and would be up soon to show him around. Jaimie had a lab jacket he would whip on in a case like that. Despite their lack of professional clothing in creative, Mr. Stevens proudly took prospective clients into the creative "den" because the full-color illustrations that came out of there were so creative and impressive.

Out of sight, behind a wall, in an alcove off the layout department, the two typesetters, Maria and Lyla, worked away on the most modern typesetting machines available. They had the new IBM Selectric typewriters. With those Selectrics, they could set type from six points to twelve points just by changing the metal ball head that rotated for each character. They could also change to serif, sans serif, or italic fonts and type as if they were using an ordinary typewriter, although, unlike a typewriter, it justified or centered text and had a memory to automatically retype something without you using the keyboard again. The machine only held that memory as long as it was turned on. Once you shut it down for the night, everything was erased.

Maria was a pretty brunette, but she had a sadness and loneliness about her. I soon learned that she hadn't been married long before her husband, a soldier, had been shipped out to Vietnam and was over there somewhere in the jungles fighting the Viet Cong. She rarely heard from him and didn't know from one day to the next if he were alive or dead. It was hard for her to watch the news each night and listen to the count of dead from the war. She never knew if he was safe with his platoon or would be coming back to her with a flag draped over his casket. They had been living in a one-bedroom apartment near Fort Belvoir before he was deployed, so she stayed working in DC even though she was alone and had no relatives in the area. She was waiting for him to return to her.

Our other typesetter was, well, kind of flirty. She was born in England and had a strong British accent. There wasn't any guy in pants that she didn't come on to. It didn't matter if he was married or not. He was man meat, and she was always hungry and preferred a fully stocked, unlimited buffet of different dishes to one single, quality choice. She was loud and raunchy and wore tight skirts and tighter sweaters and walked with a purposeful sway to her hips when she was around anything male. Her makeup consisted of heavy blue eye shadow, dark mascara, and bright red lipstick. Her equally bright red nails flashed as she typed away on the keys. Her real skill was that she was a fast and accurate typist and would have a good job without all the extra allure she threw out to the bosses. If we had a real backlog and those two were buried with work, our receptionist from downstairs would help with typesetting. I was glad they hadn't asked me to type up galleys of text, especially the reports, after I saw how boring most of it was from the government agencies. I wanted to do something more visual, more artistic.

I was getting used to my work and enjoying my job tucked back in my little corner of the room. It was challenging and exciting to be in a place full of so much energy and importance, and I was becoming a better artist. I could hardly believe I was really working in an advertising agency. I thought if I did well in layout, I might have a chance to move up in the agency and do more creative work eventually. My vantage point at my drafting desk allowed me to watch all the comings and goings in the room and out into the hallway. As I worked, I listened to the music Dean played on his small portable radio. He often tuned it to a station that played the latest hits of the '60s, and we would listen and relax to the sounds of "Blue Moon" or "Summertime" as we worked.

Two brothers worked in the photo lab downstairs in the basement of the office building. I thought it was odd that they got jobs in the same department. They would receive the artwork from technical or creative and make photographic prints of them for us to use in layout or customer presentations for approval. That way, the originals never got damaged during paste-up when they were waxed or handled and cut apart. They could also be saved and reused or modified when needed. I often did headlines for slides and overhead presentations, plus I added drawings from the technical or creative departments to those paste-ups. The guys in the photo lab downstairs would take my finished paste-up and turn it into a slide by photographing it or making it into a framed overhead projection for the clients. Everything we did was always photographed in some manner. The client never handled the originals they paid for. They were billed more for not only typesetting and preparing the artwork but also for photographing it. We kept the originals to pull back out of the file cabinets and use again. Even a minor change meant it would go through the entire process of preparing the paste-up and photographing it again so clients could be billed more.

We were so busy in our department trying to get everything done before the crushing deadlines that there was no time to socialize. Our work required focus and concentration or else serious costly mistakes could be made. Odd-numbered pages always started on the right side of a publication. If one page was wrong in a paste-up or a chart or diagram was missing, it had to be inserted back in, which might change the whole order. Sometimes a client would add something to a publication. Those alterations could throw the order of all the pages off and cause a loss of time to make it right. We never seemed to have the time needed to get any job done before a deadline without a rush. As usual, everything coming in the door arrived days late and needed to be worked on right now as if it were an emergency.

Because of the demanding workload constantly in front of me, I wasn't getting to know my coworkers. I had been packing my lunch and taking some quiet time to myself to eat at my desk. Most of the others went out to lunch daily. I didn't feel I could afford to do that yet, and they might not have wanted me to tag along.

One day, they were heading out, and Dean stopped and asked me to come along with him, Maria, and Lyla. There were several ethnic restaurants along Fourteenth Street, and that day they were going for a quick Chinese lunch. They convinced me to get away for a short while and go with them. Booker was sitting at his desk as we were leaving.

I asked him, "Aren't you escaping with the rest of us to eat Chinese today, Booker?"

It was silent as he looked back at the others and then replied, "No, I better not. I'm behind on this paste-up. I better stay here to finish it. I'll take a break later."

"Do you want me to bring something back, Booker?" Dean asked.

"Yeah, get me an order of lo mein. I'll pay you when you get back."

I was curious about what Chinese food was like. I had no idea what lo mein was but felt I would show off my ignorance if I asked.

We left the building, crossed the street, and walked south a couple of blocks. On the way, we passed a strikingly beautiful young black woman walking toward us. She was dressed tastefully in a form-fitting light gray jersey dress with a high neckline, no sleeves, and a hem that fell slightly above her kneecaps. Her dark hair fell in soft curls onto her shoulders and down her back. She walked confidently, purposefully, with her head held high as she strolled along in matching low gray heels. She had no jewelry, and the strap of a designer brown leather bag was slung over her shoulder. She was dressed stylishly and tastefully like Jackie Kennedy, I thought. This young woman had an aura or demeanor about her that demanded you pay attention to her. I heard Lyla say, "Down boy, down," to Dean after she slowly walked past us, and I wondered what that was about.

"Boy, that was a beautiful, graceful woman," I said to the group.

"Yeah, we see her here a lot," Maria answered. "She is quite lovely."

Lyla spoke up. "She's a tart, you know—a slag we call them in England. Dean's smitten with her, aren't you, Dean?" She poked Dean in the ribs with her elbow.

"No, I'm not," he answered. "I have a wife and kids, you know, and I'm happy with what I have. Besides, that guy down the street scares the hell out of me."

"What guy? Who are you talking about?" I asked.

"Her pimp, the guy sitting in that baby blue Caddie with the white sidewalls and all that shiny chrome. See him parked down there?" Dean told me pointing down the street. "Sometimes he leans on his car and just watches her."

Suddenly realizing what they were saying, I asked, "You mean that woman is a prostitute out here at noon walking the streets? I thought they only worked at night and wore skimpy clothing like miniskirts, high heel shoes, and low-cut blouses showing off their bodies. She doesn't look like a hooker. Are you sure?" I asked the group, not believing what they were saying.

Lyla asked me, "Haven't you ever heard of a man taking a long business lunch? Well, that's the business a lot of them are enjoying!"

*So, hookers roam the streets here day and night,* I thought. *Great, that puts a new slant on taking a daytime stroll.*

"I'll bet she's in great demand and makes a lot of money too," Dean said, waving his hand as if trying to cool off.

"What's the matter, Dean? The sun getting you hot?" Lyla teased.

"Quiet, Lyla," Dean told her, annoyed.

"Oh, oh, sorry, you are touchy today. You must be getting overheated," Lyla replied as Dean scowled back at her.

We reached the door to the Chinese restaurant. I had never been inside one and was interested to see what it looked like. The interior was dimly lit and decorated with red paper lanterns with tassels that hung from the ceiling. There was a large mirror along one wall with a scene of white valleys and mountains etched onto it that I assumed was a Chinese countryside. Strange music was coming from somewhere in the background.

"Wow, everything is red and gold in here," I commented.

"Yeah, it reminds me of a brothel," Lyla said, chuckling.

"Why does your mind always go there, Lyla?" Dean asked, shaking his head. "It's lunchtime. Think about something else for a change."

"Easy for you to say, Dean. You're married and probably getting all the playtime you want. Me, I have to hunt mine down," she replied.

"Well, put your gun away, Lyla. It's time for lunch, not bagging something to bang," he said.

"Oh, but Dean, if you'd have lunch with that hot babe on the street, you could have some exercise and dessert too," she said, winking at him.

"God, Lyla, give it a break, will you?" he groaned wearily. "By the way, red in Chinese culture actually stands for luck, joy, and happiness. It also wards off evil."

"Really?" Lyla replied. "Remind me never to wear red again . . . I like being evil."

We took our places at a lacquered round table. Our Chinese waitress wore a pretty silk outfit with a high collar and unusual fabric-knotted buttons that closed with loops. She handed us menus with a red cover and Chinese symbols in gold to match the rest of the room. I quickly opened it to check the prices and see how expensive the meals were. I tried to figure out what I should narrow my choices down to. I didn't know what anything was with the odd names they gave the meals like Sichuan Pork, Kung Pao Chicken, and Dim Sum. The last one sounded like an electrical problem to me.

"I have to confess," I told my coworkers, "I have no idea what to order here."

"You never had Chinese food before?" Lyla asked, raising her eyebrows.

"No, I lived in a small country town in New York. We had a family diner in the nearest town. Most of the other restaurants around the area were Italian. I'm not sure what I should be choosing," I said, blushing and embarrassed about my lack of knowledge as I studied the menu. I added, trying to be funny, "It's all Chinese to me!"

Dean, Maria, and Lyla all looked at each other and smiled.

"Boy, you really are from the boonies, aren't you?" Lyla said. Quickly, they all started making suggestions.

"You'd probably like a lo mein dish like the one Booker wants us to bring back to him," Maria suggested. "It's sort of like spaghetti with veggies but no tomato sauce."

"Oh no, you should try a stir fry. They're the best here," Lyla chimed in. "Especially the shrimp and broccoli with rice, red peppers, and bean sprouts, and that hot, spicy stir fry sauce they use. I like things hot and spicy," she said, winking at Dean again. He frowned and shook his head as he studied the menu.

"I don't know," I said. "I'm not used to my food being all stirred together."

Dean chuckled and said, "Well, I prefer the sweet and sour pork myself. Why don't we all get what we want and share some of it with Josey?" he asked the others.

"Oh, no, I couldn't let you do that. I can pay for my own food." I replied. "Taking food off someone's plate doesn't sound right to me."

"Don't be silly," Maria said gently. "We do it all the time when we eat Chinese. Just place a small order for something so you have a plate, and we'll share some of our food. Then you can find out what you like or don't like."

I had trouble understanding the waitress when she came to take our order because she had such a strong Chinese accent. Maria acted as an interpreter for me and said that I wanted an egg roll and a half order of lo mein. I only nodded and said I would drink the same thing after Maria placed her order for hot tea.

I whispered to them, "I'm sorry, I couldn't understand everything she said."

"Yeah, it's funny how some Chinese people can mess up English so much, but when it comes to paying the bill, you'll hear the price clear as a bell," Lyla joked.

Maria added, "Did you know a lot of the restaurant workers are recent immigrants from China? They're here on a work visa and are being sponsored by another family member. Most don't know English well because everyone around them speaks Chinese. Listen to them talking back in the kitchen. The immigrants can fulfill their dream of becoming American citizens by coming into the country that way. I'm glad they're here; I love Chinese food, and they add a lot to our community by being such hard and honest workers. When you come in here, it's almost like you're visiting another country."

I enjoyed meeting such different people. It was a treat to taste all the new flavors of the food my coworkers put on my plate. I decided I would order any of it again if I had the chance, especially the fried rice with bean sprouts, the General Tso's chicken, and the egg roll. The food was so different from what I was used to eating. Most of my home-cooked meals were meat, potatoes, and vegetables. I liked the crunch of the white discs they told me were water chestnuts, and those fried bean sprouts were tasty too. The deep-fried egg roll with the cabbage filling and little pieces of meat was deliciously different from the cooked cabbage rolls I made at home. Mine were made with hamburger and tomato sauce. It was the first time I met an Asian person too. I was getting more involved in the real world. A world that is full of all kinds of people with different ethnic backgrounds. I smiled when I opened my fortune cookie, which read, "*A new venture will fill your life with untold memories.*"

Earlier, Dean had turned to Maria and asked, "Are you sure you don't want to order Marty's special burger to go along with that lo mein you're eating?"

"Oh God, Dean, don't bring that up. I won't be able to finish this." She put her hand over her mouth and shuddered.

"That was an eye-opening day, wasn't it, Chickee?" Lyla said.

"Why, what happened?" I asked Dean. "What kind of special burger?"

"Tell Josey about your yummy lunch that day, Maria," Dean prodded.

"Dean, this is a warning. You're spoiling my lunch and are going to make me gag. You tell Josey if you have to. I'm still trying to forget the whole thing," Maria answered as she hunkered down and scowled at him.

Dean chuckled and said, "Well, we ordered lunch at a restaurant down the street. Marty's Place, it's called. It's a little diner tucked in between some office buildings. Maria ordered a cheeseburger and fries that day, and we were chatting and enjoying our lunch like we are now. She took a bite of her cheeseburger, then turned to say something to me when she felt something tickling her arm. She looked down to see a big roach with his antenna waving 'hi' at her as it ran up her arm towards her mouth." Dean tried to choke back a laugh.

"Dean, stop! I'm telling you again, you're going to make me gag! It wasn't that funny," Maria said.

Lyla chimed in, "Oh yes it was! You should have seen Maria's face. All the color drained out of it, and she turned white as a sheet. She shrieked, 'ROACH!' and swatted that bug off her arm so hard it sailed clear across the room and sent the other diners scrambling. She threw her cheeseburger down and ran out of the diner, and a bunch of others ran out the door too. Maria cleaned that diner out of customers. You could hear chairs loudly scraping the floor as they were being pushed back from tables and the noise of people's shoes pounding the tile as they left. It was so funny!"

Maria pleaded, "Come on, you guys, it wasn't that funny." Everyone at the table was laughing loudly now.

Dean teased, "Aww, he only wanted to take a little bite of that burger and then give you a kiss, Maria. Didn't your parents ever teach you to share?"

"Bite me," Maria said, scowling at him, and we all erupted into laughter again.

Feeling creepy, I asked, "You're telling me you have big roaches in restaurants where people eat? I thought they only existed way down south, like in Georgia and Florida."

Lyla leaned over and said, "Country Girl, there are roaches in this city big enough to put a saddle on and ride."

"You're kidding me, aren't you?" I asked.

"No, I'm not. I've seen some this big," Lyla said as she held her fingers about two inches apart to show me. I shuddered and drew in a breath as

I shook my head. Then she asked me. "Don't you have roaches and rats up in New York? I've seen pictures of rats running on the sidewalks in the news, you must have roaches there too."

"Oh, no, I lived way out in farm country in a little town called Vestal Center. I hate it when everyone calls anything above New York City just upstate New York and thinks we're like them. We are little towns and villages with names and lots of rural country, hills, streams, and lakes. It isn't just people with New York accents and skyscrapers. Did you notice I don't sound like a New Yawker?" I asked.

Maria said, "Yes, I don't hear that city sound when you speak."

Lyla continued, "And the worst part about roaches is they start crawling around your house when it's dark at night. I've heard they will crawl into your mouth if you leave it open while you're sleeping or go up your nose to get a drink. They might even tiptoe into your ear and sing you a lullaby."

Maria pleaded, "Lyla, please stop talking about roaches, I have goosebumps and my skin is crawling, and you're worrying Josey!" Turning toward me, she said, "Lyla is exaggerating, Josey. Just be sure your apartment is sprayed by an exterminator regularly, then you'll be okay."

"And do not go to greasy spoon diners like Marty's," Dean added.

As I finished my meal, I carefully looked at the stir fry before taking another bite. It was enjoyable going to lunch with them, but that was also the day they started calling me "Country Girl."

# Chapter 4

Samuel and I talked and shared more now that we had the privacy we needed in our marriage. We still stayed in touch with his mother and called to chat and find out how she was doing, but it was no longer intrusive daily reports. There were other close relatives she talked to regularly, so we knew she was safe. The move had taken a lot of the stress off Samuel's shoulders, and mine as well. He was also getting enough sleep and could watch the children during the day while I worked.

Our neighbors across the hall had recently come to DC from Lancaster, Pennsylvania, and were new to city living like us. Eli was the manager of a hardware store and had been transferred like Samuel had been. Hope, his wife, and I became fast friends and often talked while we did the wash together in the complex's laundry room. Their two girls and our two children were all close in age and had fun taking swimming lessons together and playing.

From what we had seen of Washington, DC, it was a beautiful city full of history, parks, monuments, museums, attractions, and entertainment. There were lovely, tree-lined parkways running through wooded areas that separated travelers from the busy city. Small roadside pull-offs along the Anacostia and Potomac Rivers provided a respite from the heavy traffic and a chance to view and enjoy the tranquil rivers. Often, rowing crews of men from Georgetown University practiced their teamwork on the water in pleasant weather. Attractive landscaping was everywhere along the roadways and in the parks. Lady Bird Johnson had a beautification project for the DC area and put in colorful banks of daffodils, tulips, and other plantings. Many of the federal buildings were surrounded by large beds of flowers, manicured shrubs, and different varieties of trees. The historic gray stone homes in the Georgetown area were architecturally gorgeous and helped give the city the feeling they had been there for a long time, although our country was actually a young democracy. Construction for modern, high-rise office and apartment buildings was going on just outside the downtown area, with massive cranes lifting building materials high overhead to add even more floors. There was a stark contrast of architectural styles between the old federal buildings and the sleeker glass-faced high-rises.

We could do so many activities in Washington, DC, without spending much money. We visited the Lincoln Memorial and climbed the white marble steps to read the carved inscriptions on the walls and use "Mr. Lincoln's bathrooms" in the hallways behind his statue. It was early evening, and the white marble walls surrounding his huge, seated figure had lights illuminating them. The marble was engraved with words from his Gettysburg Address and his Second Inaugural Speech. We were alone in that large open building that faced the Reflecting Pool with Mr. Lincoln's seated figure staring outward, and I read some words from the Gettysburg Address aloud. *"Four score and seven years ago, our fathers brought forth on this continent, a new nation, conceived in Liberty, and dedicated to the proposition that all men are created equal."*

I asked Samuel, "Do you know what a score is? I'm not sure."

"It's something musical, isn't it?"

"No, Samuel, I think it's a measure of time. A decade is ten years, so maybe a score is twenty? Does that sound right? It states he was speaking these words at the dedication of the Gettysburg battlefield after the Civil War. A score must be twenty years, so that would mean he was speaking eighty-seven years after our country declared its independence in 1776."

"Yes, that math works out right. A score must be twenty years."

I started to read some inscriptions again. This time from Lincoln's Second Inaugural Speech. Our young daughter, Grace, heard me say, "*with malice towards none and charity for all,*" and she asked, "What's malice, Mommy?"

"Let me think about that for a minute," I said. Then, unsure what to say, I asked Samuel, "What do you think malice is?"

His answer was, "It means you want to deck somebody."

I tried to put it into better words to help Grace understand. "Well, I believe it means you want to hurt somebody for something they did to you. To make them feel bad like you do."

"Like Daddy said, hitting them?" she asked.

"No, I think it's much worse than just wanting to hit," I told her. "It's not just the action you take or the thing you do . . . it's a feeling you have inside. You should always try to work things out with others, Grace. Try to understand why someone did something and be kind. Everyone makes mistakes and people have different opinions," I told her as I bent over and hugged her close. Someday I would tell her more about President Lincoln and the tragedy in our country regarding the Civil War and slavery. My child's innocence was too precious to burden her with that sadness now. Some grown-up issues should just wait until children are mature enough to understand.

How do you explain malice? The feeling is more than just wanting to pay someone back for a deed or hurt they inflicted on you. Malice is more sinister and evil. At the time Lincoln penned those words, he must have had the feelings aroused by the terrible tragedy of the Civil War on his mind. He knew our country was deeply divided, and Americans on both sides of the war carried hatred in their hearts for others with different ideologies and backgrounds. Families had lost loved ones, lost homes, lost lifestyles and so much more. Perhaps they suspected the deep sorrow they felt would have devoured them if they did not focus on something else, like getting revenge. So, the venom of wanting to do evil, to inflict suffering on others, became their energy to keep going. I could not know unless I had lived during those times. I only know that hatred and malice were the true enemy within them and not the remedy for their healing in our country.

Before we left the monument that evening, we threw pennies into the watery mirror of the Reflecting Pool and watched as they made ever-widening circles against the backdrop of the tall spire of the Washington Monument and the lighted walkways flanking the long rectangular pool.

On weekends, we explored Washington whenever we had the chance. On one warm weekend, we listened to the Marine Corps Band give a lively concert of John Philip Sousa tunes and other composers while we stretched out on blankets on the grass. Members of the band passed out small American flags to the crowd and then played "Stars and Stripes Forever" and "I'm a Yankee Doodle Dandy." We waved our little flags and sang right along with the crowd as that excellent band entertained us. Work kept us quite busy during the week, but on weekends we could always find something interesting to do in DC, Maryland, or Virginia.

The annual President's Cup Hydroplane races were being held at Haine's Point on the Potomac, and we headed over there one weekend to watch the boats. I asked Samuel, "Do you think President Johnson will be there to hand out the awards? It *is* the President's Cup."

"You never know, he might be. We're where he lives now. We just might get a glimpse of him," Samuel answered.

The hydroplanes were amazingly large, flat, colorful disks with a raised area for a cockpit where the driver sat. They had molded fins underneath and huge, jet-like motors propelling them on the back. When they sat still, they looked like chunky lily pads, but when they took off, high, wide white columns of water rose several feet straight up into the air behind them as if Old Faithful had suddenly erupted from their innards. You could feel the sheer power and speed of those dangerous machines skipping over the surface of the water, and their thundering noise was deafening.

As we watched them race so close to each other side by side, making sharp turns around colorful buoys, I wondered how they ever controlled those racing machines. They didn't seem tethered to the water in any way. They traveled over the surface like a flat rock skipped across a pond. Then we saw one launch its tip upwards off the water, do a backward flip, and slam onto the water's surface upside down with a loud slapping noise. The cheering crowd instantly became silent. Officials started waving red flags to the other hydroplanes as we waited for the driver to emerge from the dark water. Soon rescuers were on the scene and quickly dove beneath the boat. I heard someone close by whispering, "A couple years earlier, a driver was killed the same way." I was sure it must have certainly knocked him out at least. We collectively held our breath and soon, thankfully, this driver popped up like a released cork with the rescue divers right beside him, holding onto his arms. The crowd cheered, whistled, and clapped loudly. I shook my head in amazement and sighed with relief.

On another weekend, we hiked the wooded trails along a stream in Rock Creek Park in northern DC. Our children loved the Nature Center there and saw familiar turtles and frogs we recognized from back home. The kids watched bees coming and going from a glassed-over, active beehive and learned about the honey-making process. Several other glass enclosures held snakes. I quickly scooted the kids away from that creepy display, but Samuel pulled them back to the cages to point out the evil-looking poisonous ones with their narrow pupils and triangular heads.

He warned the children about them. "See how their colors blend in so well with what surrounds them? Look at the triangle shape of their head. Those are the worst snakes. Stay away from them. They are bad and can hurt you." Some of those reptiles did have neat patterns. It's a snake, though—that's enough for me to avoid them.

Another weekend we visited the National Mall and walked through several Smithsonian buildings. We watched in awe as an enormous, swinging pendulum swooped back and forth across the room. It was suspended from the high ceiling of the Natural History Museum. There were displays of gigantic dinosaurs, some as large as our living room, and their reassembled bodies showed their opened, toothy, skeletal mouths. You could spend hours and hours in those buildings, wandering the hallways and visiting the different floors. We stared at glass-enclosed displays of scenes from prehistoric times to the present with human and other natural and man-made artifacts.

The ruby slippers Judy Garland wore in *The Wizard of Oz* sparkled on a spotlighted, rotating display. The glittering red sequins flashed and reflected the lights positioned over them. One of the exhibits that got my attention was the violet-colored 45.5-carat Hope Diamond with its sixteen white diamonds surrounding it. The neck chain holding the gorgeous stone had forty-five white diamonds in it. That walnut-sized gem with all its facets shimmering in the light was so beautiful and heavy looking I couldn't imagine ever being comfortable wearing it. It is believed to be a piece of cursed jewelry from the beginning. A Hindu priest had stolen it from an idol in an Indian temple. Later, the jewel showed up in Europe in 1642. It has a history of people connected to it being tortured. A merchant was mauled to death by wild dogs. Thefts, suicides, murders, and other tragic events all happened in connection to that stone. No wonder it's locked up in a museum.

After some time wandering the exhibits, the eerie stillness of all the various stiff-dressed mannequins and taxidermized animal figures made us long for activity and movement. The last building we visited at the Smithsonian was the National Air and Space Museum. We had heard so much about the space race with Russia in the news that Samuel and I wanted to check that museum out. Orville and Wilbur Wright's fragile-looking plane was on prominent display there. It looked as delicate as a dragonfly with its thin wooden framework and small, fragile wheels, and I wondered how they ever got the courage to fly it.

"What do you think, Samuel? Would you have gone up in the air in that?"

"Are you kidding? If I did get it above the earth, it looks like it would just collapse into a pile of toothpicks when I landed it! Wilbur or Orville, whoever flew it, must have been a courageous man."

We moved on to see one of the space capsules that had returned to earth from orbit. Right after it had splashed down into the ocean, it was immediately retrieved by a boom on a waiting ship.

"Look at this one," I said, poking my head into the tiny space crowded with instrument panels, switches, and dials where the astronaut had sat. "There isn't any room to move in there. How did he stand it? It must have felt like being shoved into a metal garbage can with your knees up under your chin." It was eye-opening to see how small and claustrophobic those early capsules were. You could even see the heat damage on the metal shell from reentering the earth's atmosphere. They must have truly feared they might be getting cooked in an oven and could not open the door. What those astronauts had endured for our country and its space program amazed me.

Months passed quickly as we worked during the weekdays and filled our weekends with activities. Another weekend we toured the National Zoo, and the children saw exotic animals we had only seen in books or on television. Seals were splashing and barking in a pool, and the children loved the giraffes with their towering necks, long bluish tongues, and large brown patterns. The lions and tigers were scary big, much bigger than we thought they would be, and I was grateful for the heavy paned glass enclosures protecting us from them. African elephants were impressive with their size, and we all laughed as we watched them use their trunks to play with old black truck tires the keepers had put into their enclosures to encourage activity.

One Sunday, we took a trip east to picnic on the beach with Hope, Eli, and their two girls. The kids squealed and shouted as they ran in and out of the white, foamy surf. I couldn't get over how flat the landscape was. It wasn't at all like the hills I knew at home. Noisy seagulls hovered over us, looking for food they could snatch away at the first opportunity. Hope and I walked along the shore with the children, watching for shells and shark's teeth and pieces of smooth colored beach glass as Eli and Samuel trailed behind us talking. We walked together silently for a while. It was easy to get lost in our thoughts for some moments, just enjoying the sound of the ocean waves, the begging seagulls, and the laughter of our children having fun looking for shells and playing together.

The children had all gathered together, staring at something they had found. When we caught up to them, Grace asked, "What is that thing, Mommy? It looks kind of scary." I looked down to see a horseshoe crab lying on the sand. The dark brown, hard-shelled animal with its long-pointed tail did look alien. I didn't know if it was alive or dead but told the children to leave it alone and it would probably go back into the ocean. They seemed satisfied with my answer and ran on to look for more treasures.

Just like the children, Hope and I had taken off our shoes and walked barefoot on the wet gray sand where the waves were washing up onto the beach. The feeling of the moist sand underneath our feet reminded me of being a kid playing outdoors in summer. Hope's daughter ran up to her with a white sand dollar she had found. "Look, Mommy," she said, holding her hands together like an open book cradling the white disc.

"Oh, that's a special find," she told her. "You have to be very careful with that shell. It's fragile and will break easily. If it does break, though, I heard there are five tiny white doves inside. I wonder if that's true?"

"I don't want to break it, Mommy," she said, shaking her head and carefully holding the shell.

"No, you don't have to break it, honey. We'll save it just like it is and keep it in a special place. It will be a remembrance of our fun day at the beach."

"Thanks, Mommy. Here hold this. I'm going to find another one," her daughter said as she ran back to her sister to hunt for more. Hope and I just smiled at each other, seeing how happy our children were.

As we walked along the beach, we passed a young couple coming in the opposite direction. The woman was holding tightly onto her husband's arm. She leaned into him as he carried a small toddler. He wore an olive-green T-shirt with the word ARMY on it and rolled-up khaki pants. The couple looked so happy together and so in love.

After they passed, I said, "I'm glad my son is young. I hope this damn war is over before he's a teenager."

"I know what you mean, Josey. I have young brothers at home. Down here, so close to Fort Belvoir, we see soldiers on leave and recruits all the time. It's hard not to think about what's happening in the jungles overseas," she said. "So many people are tired of the war and wonder why we're even fighting so far away. I know we're fighting over there to keep from fighting our enemies in our own country, and I do honor the soldiers. However, that country is half a world away and so separated from us. I sometimes wonder if we should be putting our young men and women in harm's way like that. If it's worth it."

"You do know, Hope, they're protecting our diplomats and other Americans working over there too, don't you? They're fighting to keep that country from being taken over by the communists. The Viet Cong are killing a lot of innocent people."

"I know, I know. It's an honorable cause for our country to defend and protect democracy for people that don't have the resources to defend themselves from such overwhelming, powerful enemies. But we're sending some of our best young men and women to that war. They're the future leaders of our country, full of talent, ideals, and so much potential."

"Robert Kennedy said something in a speech the other day that was food for thought. I can't quote him exactly, but I think he said. '*We can't, and should not, take it on as the job of the United States to put down disorder and internal violence everywhere in the world.*' He said he didn't think that was the mission of the United States. That's something to think about. What's your view on that, Hope?"

"There are some conflicts in this world that I think we must get involved in like we had to in World War II. But no, I don't think we should be getting in the middle of every country's politics. Our own country has people suffering and needing help, and our resources can only be stretched so far. Our taxes are high now. Plus, we're losing so many of our precious young men and women to war, or they're coming home maimed and mentally broken. I know we're supposed to be the leaders and defenders of democracy. But it just doesn't seem right that we're involved in so many foreign countries. We seem to be spread all over," she said. We walked on in silence, thinking of all the American soldiers fighting in the jungles and serving in other places in the world while we freely enjoyed a stroll along the beach with our family on a sunny day. Maybe that was exactly why our soldiers were fighting.

Samuel and Eli had stopped to talk to a fisherman, and we joined them. Eli asked him how the fishing was and what bait he used. He reached into a container and pulled out something called a bloodworm. The children all shouted, "Ew! Yucky!" together when they saw its squirming body. It was the biggest, ugliest worm I had ever seen, with fleshy, dark, hooklike barbs all over its body. When the fisherman held it up by one end, the other end became a fat bulbous mass full of blood. It was disgusting, and when we walked on, I vowed I would never fish with anything like that for bait.

It was a wonderful day. We returned home from that trip with happy memories and pockets full of "treasures" to admire again later.

We took a trip back to the National Mall to see the cherry trees when they were blooming and spread out our hands and caught the pink petals that fell when a breeze blew as we wandered the sidewalks underneath them. We were reminded of how much DC is an international city as we walked among residents from different parts of the country and visitors from all over the world. We heard people speaking to each other in languages that were strange to us. We stopped at one of the multiple beds of daffodils that Lady Bird Johnson had planted around Washington, and the kids stuck their noses into the yellow blooms and smelled springtime in flower. We laughed when we noticed Lucas had yellow pollen on his nose like a honeybee.

That night we returned home with our minds full of all the new and exciting experiences we were having.

Our hometown only had one local airport with a short runway for small commuter jets and passenger planes. Those planes held six people at most, but here the jets were massive and full of people. They were constantly flying overhead, arriving and departing every few minutes. We parked our car in a landscaped area near the end of a runway at Kennedy International Airport and got out, then we all laid down on the grass facing the sky. Huge planes came barreling down the runway and lifted off right over us. The noise of the jets was so deafening we couldn't talk over it. We felt the ground under us vibrate from the weight of the heavy, moving jets on the runway. When they lifted off, we could see the pilots in the cockpit and read the numbers on the underside of the plane. It was so close we could even see the shiny heads of the rivets that pinned the plane's metal skin together. The kids loved it and waved at the people looking down from the plane's windows; some even waved back. Our children clapped and shouted as if they had just been given a Christmas present. It was a thrill for rural people like us who had only seen jets leaving white trails far above us in the sky. Where were all those people going on their journeys, we wondered.

Hope and I spent a lot of time together talking every day. We were folding clothes in the laundry room and chatting, as usual, when I told her, "I have to tell you something that's bothering me, Hope. You've seen Lucas playing with his yellow Tonka dump truck, the one he loves so much and likes to sit on and pretend to drive, right? Well, it was stolen right off our patio last night! Someone actually came close to our back-door and took it while we were sleeping inside. We never had to worry about anything getting stolen from our yard at home. We never even locked our doors. That makes me uneasy and angry."

"You're kidding! I had something stolen too," she said. "I came back to the laundry room last week to take my clothes out of the dryer, but someone had gotten there before me, and my things were scattered all over. Some of my sweaters and jeans were gone. The creepy part is they took some of my underwear too. I couldn't believe it! We're living with thieves at this complex, Josey. Be careful with everything," she told me as she shook her head. "Unbelievable. You can't trust people anymore; this is a different world." We were both silent for some time, thinking about how we had to keep our guard up in this place. Before we left, we warned each other again to be careful and watch our belongings.

Most of the children at the apartments spent time swimming in the large rectangular pool behind our apartment building. I could easily see the pool right out our glass doors. It was just across the sidewalk and lawn from our garden apartment on the bottom floor. The children living at the apartments also liked to play in the "woods" on the other side, just beyond the pool. It was only a cluster of thick trees and bushes on a small hillside but nice because that knoll was tall enough and wide enough to block the view of all the streets and buildings beyond it. Looking out our windows, we saw the blue-green water of the large pool sparkling in the sun and then a wooded area. It made us feel like we weren't right in the middle of a busy cosmopolitan city. Sitting on our deck, soaking up the sunshine, we watched the kids playing hide and seek and cowboys and Indians over there with their friends. Even when they were out of sight among the trees and bushes, we could hear their familiar voices, and they would answer us back, "I'm right here, Mommy," and wave when we called out to check on them.

There were shallow dips and raised humps all over that knoll. The kids thought they were small hideouts and had fun playing in them. Grace and Lucas brought a small animal bone back from their play and said, "Look, Mommy, it's a dinosaur bone just like we saw in the Smithsonian

Museum." They were so proud of their find, even though we knew it was most likely an animal bone. We set their treasure aside on the windowsill. Soon other children started bringing small bones back from their play as well. We weren't concerned until one of them brought back a skull and handed it to his mother, saying, "Look at this neat skull I found. Can we use it for Halloween?" He was so pleased with what he had found. His mom almost fainted when he handed it to her and she realized it was an actual human skull.

The police were called to investigate the "woods," and we found out it was an old cemetery. The officer told us gravediggers had recently opened the graves and exposed the skeletons.

"Why would they ever be doing something like that?" I asked the policeman.

"Ma'am, they rob the dead of any jewelry the bodies were buried with. They work mostly at night," he answered as he wrote up his report. "Desperate people do desperate things around here," he added.

It frightened me that a strange man or men, especially grave robbers, had been over there where my children played every day. The neighborhood was getting scarier to me, with thieves and gravediggers nearby. What else was going on that I didn't know about? I started paying much, much closer attention to everything around us, not just our belongings but our precious children too.

Not long after that, I had another eye-opening experience. The drive to work every day was so stressful. There were so many commuters jamming the streets, all at the same time, that traffic was horrible. It angered me every time I had to stop and wait for an opening to go around those double-parked limousines by the embassies. Why couldn't they respect our traffic laws? I had tried taking other streets but got very lost one day, so I returned to using the familiar route past that area. Our other problem was Samuel didn't have a car each day because I had to use it. I decided I would ride the bus to work instead.

The morning I stepped onto that bus, I stepped into a different world. Every face staring back at me was black. People leaned out toward the aisle to get a better look at me. All of them stared as if they just saw an alien in their midst. I had already put my money in the metal box by the bus driver. I was committed to that transport, so I needed to sit down. I eased my way down the aisle to about halfway back and was relieved to find an empty seat. The bus driver had watched me in the rearview mirror, making sure I had sat down before he took off. I slid over next to the window and hunkered down as the bus traveled on. Looking forward, I noticed some ladies were dressed in uniforms as if they were domestic help. Most of the men looked as if they were in some type of service job, and a few dressed like office workers.

I felt so out of place. I didn't think I was superior, though. I had worked cleaning houses for others and had been a waitress in my teens. I felt like I was injecting myself into a world that was so different from mine. A world I didn't know anything about. I stared out the bus window and watched the buildings and streets we traveled past. The bus was eerily quiet, as if everyone was resting up for a trying day ahead. At the next stop, an older black woman got on and sat down next to me. We said "hello," and then neither of us spoke again. When the bus came to her stop, she got up and left. I carefully watched the street signs for my stop near the agency. The last thing I wanted to do was get off on the wrong block. When I did get off the bus, the driver said, "You have a good day now." I thanked him. I think he knew I had felt so out of place.

When I mentioned the bus ride to Booker at work, he said, "Welcome to the city, Country Girl . . . You didn't know the buses are filled with black people?" Then he chuckled while he shook his head. I suffered in silence again on the bus ride back home. *Why am I the only white person on the bus? Am I imagining a hint of hostility in the faces of some passengers? Or is my fear of their difference making me sense something that isn't there? Is my presence on the bus unwelcome?* I couldn't help but wonder, did a black person feel that uncomfortable when they're surrounded by a group of strange white people?

I started driving myself to work again the next day.

Samuel's job was going great. He was learning new skills as a fuel injection specialist, and they trusted his abilities enough to send him on road calls to fix trucks that had broken down on the highway. We had replaced some furniture we had sold by shopping at a local Goodwill store. We were still tight for money to meet the utility bills and pay our apartment rent plus other expenses though and had to watch our pennies. I had come home one day to a hangtag on our doorknob warning us about our late rent. It was embarrassing, and I quickly ripped it off and hoped no one else had seen it on their way to the laundry room.

Samuel told me he had to join the International Association of Machinists and Aerospace Workers Union for his job, and they would be automatically taking dues out of his paycheck from now on.

"Samuel, you worked for the same company up north and never had to join the union. Why do you have to join a union here?" I asked.

"That wasn't a union shop up north. I haven't got a choice; all the mechanics here are union members. I can't continue to work in that shop unless I join."

"But what good is joining a union going to do? Does that mean that if they strike at the shop you won't get paid?" I asked worriedly. "That sounds like a big union too. It includes the aerospace workers. If the pilots or airplane mechanics went on strike, would you have to also? Is that how it works?"

"No, I don't think that will ever happen," he answered, trying to ease my worry. "Sometimes these companies won't listen to a worker's complaints or treat them fairly. But if employees get together as a group, they can get things changed. Besides, the dues are to help get us money if the group did go on strike. I don't like it any more than you, Josey. It's supposed to be for the good of the workers. I have no choice, hon, I have to join," he said, stroking my back. "At least they have great benefits at this company, and my boss is a good guy."

"I just get tired of bureaucrats taking money out of our pockets for one thing or another. It adds up, and we need every dollar we earn. You work so hard."

"We'll be okay," he said as he kissed my forehead, the side of my face, my lips, and pressed his body close to me.

"Samuel, stop trying to change the subject. I'm trying to talk to you about something serious," I said, nudging him away and turning my back.

He reached out, wrapped his arms around me, and pulled me close to his body. "But, Josey, don't worry so much, hon. We'll be okay. Just feel how well we fit together. No more talking now," he said, then whispered in my ear, "The kids are asleep. Let's go to bed and take our minds off our troubles for a while."

"Our bills Samuel . . . we need . . . we have to . . ." My voice trailed off as he tenderly kissed me. My mind was shutting down. I gladly went with him as he pulled me toward our bedroom. I needed to forget the bills, my work, and the problems that had worried me so much that week.

Chapter 5

Much of the work we did at the agency was for different federal government divisions. I often did paste-ups on publications with "CONFIDENTIAL" stamped in bold letters on every page. Usually, it was something boring. They were often pages and pages of mundane reports that included black and white charts and graphs from the technical department and even more pages of text analyzing statistics. None of it was interesting enough to hold my attention without starting to yawn, and I wondered how the civil servants who wrote the stuff could stand it.

I had been working on my new job for a few months when our proofreader, Priscilla, announced she was having a party for all of us at the place she rented in Georgetown. I wasn't sure if Samuel and I should attend. We probably could get Hope to watch the kids for one night. However, I hesitated because neither Samuel nor I had done much socializing or party-going, and we had never been to a cocktail party. We were unsure about what to expect. I thought we should attend because it seemed important for my work and getting along with my coworkers. I didn't want to offend anyone by being absent. I was also curious and wanted to know more about the people I worked with.

The party was scheduled for "sevenish." After going up and down the Georgetown neighborhood street several times, we managed to squeeze our Chevy into a parking space between all the Lincolns and Cadillacs near the address Priscilla had given us. We walked down the sidewalk toward the house number she had given me and admired the big, well-maintained, greystone homes we passed. We found the place Priscilla rented. It was large and impressive, and she had told me she had the use of one whole floor of it. It wasn't just a house; it was a mansion.

"God, this place must be expensive to rent," Samuel said as he looked at the large, impressive stone building. "Glad we're not paying rent on this museum every month."

"I don't understand how she does it, Samuel. She can't make that much money at the agency, can she?" I asked. "She's a proofreader, although that is one of the most important jobs there."

We continued up the marble sidewalk, past the neatly manicured landscaping, up the stone steps, to the portico landing, and rang the bell. Warm lights streamed out the windows, and you could hear music and conversations inside. Priscilla opened the door with a half-empty drink in her hand. "Josey, good, you came. I wasn't sure you would."

"Priscilla, this is Samuel, my husband. Samuel, this is Priscilla. She's my friend from work who invited us to this beautiful home tonight."

Priscilla switched hands with her drink and shook Samuel's. "Glad to meet you Shamyule. Whoops!" She laughed. "I mean Sam-u-el," she said, pronouncing his name more carefully. "Come on in here, you two, and join the party."

I whispered under my breath as she turned and walked away. "Someone's way ahead of us on the drinks."

Priscilla announced, "Look everyone, Country Girl is here with her husband, Sam-u-el." The room was full of my coworkers, who turned and raised their glasses or waved at us. Then they returned to their conversations.

"Follow me. We've set up a bar. You have to get a drink," Priscilla said. "Some of us are a little ahead of you already." She refilled her glass as Samuel and I looked at each other and smiled when she echoed my whispered remark. Pointing to the dining table, she said, "There are some hors d'oeuvres over there. Make yourself at home. I have to go ask Booker something. Please excuse me." With that, she left us standing there alone.

Samuel examined the bottles at the well-stocked bar. "Do you see a beer anywhere?" he asked, looking around.

"No, it seems this is all they have, hon. I guess they go for the hard stuff in this town. Remember that you're driving, please," I said and asked him to pour me some red wine. Samuel chose something for himself.

We hadn't gone to college and had little experience with hard liquor or parties like this one. We didn't know what we were doing. He put some alcohol in a glass and added lots of mixers. We wanted to feel like one of the crowd with a drink in our hands. This was a new experience for us, trying new things and blending in when possible. We wandered over to the hors d'oeuvres table to see what was there. A huge bouquet of white lilies and pink roses sat in the middle of a large round table. It was surrounded by several silver trays of delicious-looking food. The floral arrangement was certainly created by a professional designer.

I nudged Samuel in the ribs when I saw a tray of crackers with something black on top of them. "Is that caviar on those crackers, Samuel?"

"Damn if I know," he said. "I've never seen caviar on crackers before, and I'll be damned if I'm going to eat it either. It's fish eggs, you know. We use the red ones to bait Steelhead Trout back home. Damn, they eat bait here and they call us unsophisticated," he said, laughing. "Next thing you know, they'll be putting crawly worms on those crackers."

"Shh . . ." I tried to get him to lower his voice. "Don't let my coworkers know how ignorant we are about this stuff, please."

I chose a couple of small pieces of a green melon wrapped with paper-thin ham that looked tasty and took some large shrimp surrounding a bowl of a creamy mixture to dip it in. I added a couple of stuffed mushrooms to my small plate and looked at Samuel. He was heaping everything he could onto his plate.

"Don't take so much, Samuel. It's supposed to be only a taste, not a meal. Go easy on it," I told him quietly.

"I'm hungry. We skipped supper to make it here on time, remember?" He smiled at me and asked, "Where are the sandwiches and chips?

And where in hell are we supposed to sit? It looks like they took most of the chairs out of the room. The few seats that are left are already taken."

"Samuel, you're supposed to hold your drink in one hand and balance your plate in the other. Every once in a while, put your drink down and take a bite, and please don't forget to talk to people. Look around and mimic what the others are doing, okay? We got this. It's important for my work, dear; we should mix and socialize," I said quietly.

The truth is, I didn't know what to do either. But I was going to try to fit in with my coworkers. My party experiences consisted of birthday parties, family picnics, and baby showers. We took a few nibbles of our food and swallowed a couple of sips of our alcohol, which relaxed us both. We stood together silently, taking in the surroundings. The decorating was something you would see in the photos of an interior design magazine. Expertly tailored satin drapes hung on the large floor-to-ceiling windows and puddled on the rug. People lounged on beautifully carved wood furniture with silky fabrics and decorative pillows. Large, heavy mirrors and works of art adorned the walls and were complemented by small statues and bouquets of fresh flowers here and there on gilded side tables.

At first glance, the interior of the room had looked simple. However, when you looked closer at all the details, you could tell it was all expertly decorated with quality furnishings. Priscilla breezed by on her way to the bar. I told her how beautiful the place was.

"Do you live here by yourself, Priscilla?" I asked. "This is a lovely home."

"No, Jen is my roommate. She's over there talking to Cade." She looked at them then frowned and added, "Looks like she might need a break too. Come on, I'll introduce you." She took my arm and led us over to them. Samuel followed along reluctantly, still nibbling his food.

"Jen, this is Josey—we call her Country Girl—and her husband, Samuel. Oh, and this is Cade," she said, motioning to us. "He works at the agency with the rest of this bunch," Priscilla said. The two men shifted their drinks and shook hands.

Everyone took a sip of their drink. Then Jen asked, "So, how do you like DC, Josey?"

We chatted about all the things to do and see in the area. We discussed where we had lived before for a few minutes, then Jen excused herself and left us alone with Cade. I had the feeling she was grateful to get away.

Cade had never been a friendly person at work. He was from the technical department, and I hadn't spoken to him much. There was an awkward silence as we sipped our drinks and looked around the room. Cade took a pull on his cigarette and slowly blew smoke rings. Then, he flicked the ash onto the expensive rug. I frowned, ignored his lack of common courtesy, and stifled the urge to drop to my knees and clean up the ashes. Instead, I cleared my throat and asked him, "Cade, how did you end up working at AdArt&Tech?"

"I attended community college for technical drafting, and when I graduated, the student services office found me a job there. I've been at the agency for about six years now."

"Were you raised in this area?"

"Raised here in DC? Are you kidding? No one is raised here in DC unless you're a . . ." He paused and took a big gulp of his drink and continued. "Well, let me put it this way. Everyone with a decent job in DC is from somewhere else."

"Where are you from originally?" I asked him, wondering.

"I'm from Virginia, over past Fairfax way, a different country from around here," he said, scanning the room.

Remembering the heavy traffic of cars and tractor-trailers on the Beltway and the backups that would happen at the entrance and exit ramps, I asked him, "It must take you a long time to get to work each day, doesn't it?"

"Yeah, but it's worth getting away from the city to live out there. Much safer, a different class of people. I've got a great car for cutting in and out of the hellish traffic. I can get around those dumbasses that hold things up every day by going way too slow. Stupid idiots," he added.

Samuel was munching on his hors d'oeuvres while looking around the room and not listening as I tried to make conversation with Cade.

"Oh, what kind of car do you drive?" I asked, trying to keep some sort of conversation going.

"I've got a red Mustang, all souped up," he said, taking another drag on his cigarette. He flicked the ashes onto the rug again, then rocked back on his heels.

*Well, stiff and boring Cade has a wild side,* I thought, then I remembered the car I had seen my first day of work in the parking lot. Cade owned the red car with the big rebel flag on its bumper.

Cade didn't seem interested in knowing us any better and didn't ask us anything about our lives. He didn't even turn and reply to me when I talked to him. I had to speak to the side of his face. I was merely a noise in his ear. He kept looking around the room and seemed fixated on what Jen was doing. Perhaps he was hoping to hook up with her or another woman. I wasn't sure, but he was a dull person to hang out with at a party or anywhere else.

I scanned the room for faces I recognized and saw Dean, Lyla, and Maria chatting together over in the corner and laughing. Not far away, Ted Wickham stood with a woman I didn't recognize.

"Who's that woman with Ted?" I asked Cade.

"Oh, that's his wife. She's quite the bitch. One of those high-maintenance types no man wants to get stuck with, no matter rich or how good the sex is," he answered, sneering. "Look at her, so smug and uppity. Can you imagine her ever getting hot and sweaty in bed? I don't think so! It might ruin her manicure," he answered and took a big swallow of his drink.

I blushed vividly at his frank comments and stepped further away from him. I wasn't liking the Cade I was getting to know. Ted's wife did seem kind of cold, and seeing them standing together, you could tell they certainly weren't having a good time. On the other hand, the creative department artists were the life of the party. They were loud, funny, and colorful. One of them was passing a cigarette around and talking loudly. The men had worn the new hippie-style outfits with white bell-bottomed pants and colorful vests. Their shirts were open halfway down to show off their big peace sign jewelry hanging on metal chains. They even had headbands on, and one person had painted a peace sign on his cheek.

Samuel nudged my arm. "Josey, do you work with a bunch of Flower Children? Check out those women. They even have daisies in their hair."

I looked at their dates more closely and saw they were wearing peasant-style blouses with long, flowing, colorful skirts, sandals, more peace sign jewelry, and headbands. They did resemble the Flower Children I had seen in the news stories from California. Students were participating in sit-ins and protests against the war out there. The evening news showed their sit-ins every night and the police trying to disperse them.

"No, I don't work with them. Only the guys, although they all do look like hippies tonight too."

"Hey, maybe those girls will strip naked and start dancing around," Samuel said. "They believe in freedom of their bodies and pursuing joy, don't they?"

"Dream on, Samuel," I told him. "That's not going to happen tonight. At least I don't think it's going to and if it does we're leaving!"

"Did you see them passing that cigarette around?" he asked me. "I think they're 'expanding their consciousness,' so they call it, with weed too," he added.

That cigarette did seem suspicious. I watched as Jaimie walked over to the record player and put a 45 record on. It was "Born to Be Wild" by Steppenwolf, and he cranked up the volume and yelled, "Time to dance, everyone!" He reached out to one of the hippie girls, pulled her close, and started dancing with her.

I looked at Samuel, wondering if we should dance too. He read my mind and shook his head no at me. He was still munching on his pile of hors d'oeuvres and only wanted to watch the others. I silently prayed, *please, God, don't let Cade ask me to dance.* The thought must have never entered his mind because he stood there like a statue staring at the room while continuing to smoke. I noticed his gaze followed Jen's activities again. She was having a blast, twirling and dancing with one of the artists. Ted Wickham and his wife held each other stiffly apart, not even looking into each other's faces. Dean danced with Lyla while holding her at arm's length. Maria sat in a chair and stared out the window. She had that sad gaze on her face again. *I'll bet she's wondering what her husband is doing right now in Vietnam*, I thought. *Damn war, taking so many away from the people who love them.*

The music changed to "Strangers in the Night." It was a slow dance song, and the couples danced closer to each other.

Suddenly, Cade shouted. "Well, will you look at that shit!" he said, shaking his head. I followed the direction of his gaze to see Priscilla dancing close to Booker, my black coworker from the layout department.

"Some people have no taste. Others just don't know their place," he said.

As I watched, Priscilla, now very drunk, leaned against Booker. It looked like she was a rag doll in his arms, and he was holding her up. Booker looked uncomfortable with her slumping against him, and his eyes met Cade's, who muttered, "Disgusting." Cade tipped his head back, finished off his drink, and wiped the back of his hand across his mouth. It didn't bother me that Booker and Priscilla danced together. They were friends from work, but it obviously crossed some line in Cade's narrow mind.

Though we'd only been there a short while and hadn't mingled much, Samuel whispered that he thought we should leave. "I'm not feeling this socializing thing," he said. I felt the same way too. I wasn't comfortable in that room. I introduced him to Dean, Maria, and Lyla before we left, and we quietly slipped away while everyone was busy dancing and walked out into the cool evening air.

"Guess I learned a little more than I wanted to about my coworkers, Samuel. Maybe I'm just not cut out for partying and socializing."

"I know I'm not after seeing that crowd. You work with that weird bunch? I'll bet Cade is fun to be with every day," he said. "He should have been named Richard. "

"Why is that?" I asked Samuel.

"Because he's a real Dick!" he answered.

"Samuel!" I said, punching his arm.

"Well, he is," he repeated under his breath, then he added, "And a man could starve to death eating food like that." He put his arm around my shoulder. "Let's stop someplace before we go home and get a pizza with the works."

"Sounds good to me, and yes, Cade is a Dick." We laughed together as we walked hand in hand to our car.

* * *

Later that night, Samuel and I were lying in the dark, talking about the party and our day before falling asleep. "Boy, you work with a strange mix of people, Josey," he told me.

"Yes, I guess I do, but they're interesting. I'm just not sure if I want to get to know them all better after tonight. I've learned enough about Cade for sure. How about the people you work with at your shop? What are they like?"

"They're mostly good guys. One of the black mechanics, Tommy, is such a hard worker. He does twice the work most other guys do and doesn't complain, no matter what the bosses throw at him. I guess he's got a big family to take care of. God, that guy can work, and he's fast too," Samuel said. "We eat lunch together lots of days, and he just wants the same things for his family that we do, to have a good life and raise our kids to be decent human beings."

"Does he live in Washington?" I asked Samuel.

"No, he said he has a nice home over in Glen Arden, Maryland, and has a heck of a drive to work," Samuel answered. "He comes that far because he gets better pay with benefits here."

"We only have one black person working at the agency, and that doesn't seem right to me. I wonder why that is? Surely there must be others capable of working there. How about your shop, is it mostly white mechanics there?" I asked.

"No, I'd say it's a pretty equal mix. We even have a guy from Puerto Rico and another from Mexico. Our boss is fair about hiring people. I believe he hires on abilities. The guys were talking about that at lunch one day. They say some places down here see color first before anything else. There are still plenty of places where only white people need to apply for a job. Anybody else won't be hired. Mack Trucks isn't like that," Samuel said.

"Does everybody get along okay?" I asked him.

"Well, for the most part. There are two mechanics who get on each other's nerves at times. I think one of these days they're going to have it out."

"What's their problem?" I asked him.

"Everything, actually. I think the one guy is into that new black power movement and the other is a southern redneck and they just can't stand each other, and everyone knows it. They spend so much time swearing at each other and calling insults that it keeps things stirred up between them. They're like two roosters in a barnyard. It's so bad, the boss makes sure they aren't working in bays next to each other. Most of us working there share tools like wrenches we might not have, but those two would never share anything. They're always accusing each other of stealing tools instead. The rest of the guys get along well, though. They realize they have a good job and don't want to screw it up," Samuel said. "I think they don't get fired because there's a shortage of skilled diesel mechanics. I guess that's why I got a job here."

"You're not taking sides with anyone, are you, Samuel? We don't know these people very well, and taking sides could be a mistake."

"Me? No way! Those two can quarrel all they want, just don't bring me into it. I guess they've been butting heads and putting each other down for so long they don't know how to stop. I totally ignore them and do my job."

We were both quiet for a few minutes, then I asked him. "Did you hear what Robert Kennedy's campaign slogan is?"

Sleepily and somewhat annoyed at being kept awake, he asked, "No, what is it?"

"His slogan is, and I hope I get it right: '*Some men see things as they are and ask why. I dream of things that never were and ask why not.*' I think it's meant to be about a lot of things—ending poverty and racial injustice and having peace in the world among them."

Samuel said, "From what I've seen and heard of him, I think he'd make a good president if he gets elected." Then, yawning, he said, "I'm kinda tired, Josey."

"Yes, I think so too, Samuel. He really does care about people. He took a trip to Kentucky to visit a country school there. Cronkite showed pictures of him in a one-room schoolhouse that was only heated by a potbellied stove. It even had an outhouse behind the building, like some schools our grandparents attended. The kids were frightened to see all the strange people with camera lights flashing at them and everything. Bobby knelt by their desks and spoke quietly to them, one at a time, asking them if they had anything to eat that day. He was also interested in what they had for books and school supplies. I thought we had it hard back in the country growing up. After seeing those kids and how little they had, I realized we're blessed, Samuel. There's crippling poverty in the United States. It's shocking in this day to have so much of that in our country. Aren't we supposed to be a wealthy nation?"

I continued, "You know, Bobby Kennedy came from wealth and privilege and could have isolated himself from political service and everything like that. His family was already famous because of his brother John, and they were rich. He probably could get elected without getting involved with helping the poor and those fighting segregation. Instead, he chose to serve our country as an attorney general and now a presidential candidate. His family has been serving in politics for a long time. I think he cares about many things. Did you know that when he was attorney general, he sent federal troops to Mississippi to enforce the Supreme Court order to admit the first black student to the University of Mississippi?" I asked Samuel.

"Uh-huh," Samuel mumbled with his back turned and yawned loudly again.

"Johnson announced his War on Poverty four years ago and then basically did nothing. He's so far over his head in this Vietnam War issue, he's drowning, and Lady Bird, she must have a war on poor landscaping because she's planting flowerbeds everywhere. She wants masses of flowers for masses of people, and don't get me started on this school segregation stuff," I added.

"Oh, I don't think the problem is getting you started, Josey," Samuel mumbled. "The problem is getting you to—"

I interrupted him before he could finish his sentence. "What's wrong with this country? We have money to spend on daffodil bulbs but can't get a poor child in Kentucky a textbook or a meal?"

"Josey?"

"It isn't right, is it, Samuel? Where are our priorities as a country?"

"Josey? Can you stop talking so we can go to sleep?"

"Samuel, do you think we're prejudiced?"

"What? No . . . how could we be? We've never lived around any other races before we moved here or went to school with people who looked much different than us. We had a big population of people with Italian heritage in our area, but that was all. We can't be prejudiced," Samuel answered sleepily, yawning some more.

"But maybe that's just how you get to be prejudiced. You're basing your opinions on remarks by others, or jokes, or television, which only shows harmful stuff. Maybe some relative brought their prejudice back to the family like an ant carries poison back to the ant hill. Even the books we read as a child could have influenced us negatively. I remember reading *Little Black Sambo* and looking at the pictures in it when I was young. I thought all black people looked like him. See what I mean, Samuel? Unless you get to know someone personally and see what their lives are really like, you may form a wrong opinion of them not based on reality. Think of all the dumb blonde jokes you've heard over the years. Didn't that make you think all blondes might be dumb? But they aren't. Lots of them aren't even really blonde."

Samuel turned over and spoke. "Yes, Josey, I see what you're saying and agree with you. Now, is there a switch on you somewhere I can throw so we can go to sleep? I need to turn you off!"

Josey gave him a quick kiss and replied. "Yes, dear. I love you. Good night." She was silent for a few moments, then added, "It just really gets me all fired up, though. It's so unfair that some must suffer and go without like those little children in Kentucky while others have so much."

# Chapter 6

It was easy to observe the day-to-day activities of my coworkers from my desk in the back corner of the room. At times, I could hear Dean talking lovingly to his wife or children on the phone.

"You mind Mommy now," he was saying gently but firmly. "She told you to make your bed and pick up your clothes, didn't she? When Daddy gets home, I expect to see your room all clean and neat, okay? You want your allowance this week, don't you? Daddy loves you, now put Mommy back on."

Then a pause. "Yes, dear, I told her. I hope your day goes better now. No, I don't have to work late. A pot roast—that sounds good. See you later. Love ya too. Yes, later babe. Bye." Dean hung up the phone, looked at us, then said, "Crisis averted on the home front." He took a deep breath, then he took some finished pages off the top of the growing pile on his desk and started checking them for accuracy.

We chuckled and got back to work. I could tell Dean was a good father and a devoted husband. Maria and Lyla talked quietly in their alcove at times, and when they weren't speaking, you could hear the steady staccato of the IBM Selectric typewriters as they typed galleys of copy. I was getting to know the typesetters better. I had learned from Lyla's remarks that she was always on the prowl for a man. She was single and often filled us in on whatever loser she was dating at the time. She must have been choosing from the same throwaway pile because they all seemed to follow a repeated pattern. She would date a guy for a few weeks, which for Lyla meant he would move into her apartment right away. Soon, he would get jealous of her flirting with another man. There would be a huge fight, and she would throw him out to pick up the next one.

Lyla was into the new "free love" movement. Traditional dating and marriage were no longer the trendy way of having a relationship for her. The evening news was reporting stories about "swingers" and "cougars" and other unconventional relationships. The new modernism was shocking to many. Tradition and morals were being set aside for exploration, personal satisfaction, and fulfilling fantasies. Lyla was enjoying all those new freedoms. The popular music on the radio reflected the disruption in morality with songs like "Light My Fire" and "Stoned Soul Picknic." Everything we understood as normal and expected moral behavior in our lives was in tremendous upheaval and flux as it was redefined: in our homes, on our streets, on campuses, and in our government.

Maria wasn't talkative and kept busy focusing on doing her job. She had a small picture of her soldier-husband sitting on her desk. Sometimes I'd see her looking at his photo with her hands hovering motionless over her keyboard, while her thoughts were of him in Vietnam. She was so lonely and in need of comforting. I just wanted to hug her myself when I saw her sad eyes. I wanted to tell her he would be okay, but no one could guarantee that.

I noticed Ted Wickham started taking the copy to be typeset directly to Maria and bypassing handing it to Dean first. When Ted gave Maria the copy, he would lean in close to her as he pointed out typesetting markups on the papers. Sometimes his hand lingered on her back or he'd rest it on her shoulder. That was happening more often. Then I understood clearly when I saw her eyes as she turned and looked up at him. Not long after that, Maria started skipping lunch with us. Her excuse was that she had to finish typing some work that had a tight deadline.

I began to wonder if something else was going on. We returned from lunch earlier than usual one day, and Ted and Maria came back into the room together, laughing.

They both looked so happy but embarrassed when they saw us already back from lunch. Ted volunteered that he had to show Maria something down in the photo lab about a galley. But we could tell they had gone out some place together. We all realized they were having an affair. I wasn't bothered with them being together, even though it would probably not end well. It was their business, their life, not mine. Maria adored her husband but was so painfully lonely. She needed someone to wrap their arms around her. She needed tenderness in a world that was being so cruel while she worried and waited for her husband to return.

And Ted, I had seen his wife at the cocktail party, and she had visited him at work a couple of times. She was a cool one and definitely did not care how stressful Ted's job was as long as he made lots of money for her to spend on those designer clothes she wore, the expensive car she drove, and the prestigious home they had in the hills of Virginia. They had no children, and Ted needed the arms of a warm woman as much as Maria needed his arms sheltering her. I didn't think it would ever go any further than that. They were two people showing love and comfort to each other at a time when they both needed it. Ted's face even had a more relaxed, happy look, and I didn't see that awful tick so often.

Booker was still somewhat of a mystery to me. He often went in and out of the room leaving his work sitting on his drafting desk. One day he returned to the room and asked, "Josey, do you have an envelope, any envelope?"

"What do you need an envelope for?"

"I just need it; do you have one or not?" he asked again, sounding a little irritated. I looked through my desk and checked my briefcase.

"No, I'm sorry, Booker. I don't have one. Why do you need it?" I asked again.

"I just do. It's for the guys in creative," he said.

"Maybe the receptionist has one," I told him.

"No, I better not ask her," he replied. He looked disappointed as he left the room.

Booker often had bloodshot eyes, and I wondered why. Did he stay up late watching the television? Now, with his request for the envelope, I wondered if he was smoking marijuana and sharing it with the guys in creative or possibly using something else. Then I dismissed that thought. I liked Booker and wanted to know more about his background. I wondered what his life was like growing up. It was certainly different than mine. There was so much controversy right now regarding segregation in schools and housing. I was interested in knowing his thoughts and what his experiences had been. Unfortunately, it was difficult to do much talking, and he never came to lunch with us. Every day, our busy work environment kept us focusing and concentrating on what we had to finish before a deadline. There was no time for chit chat while working.

Jaimie was an interesting character. He did the illustrations and photo retouching of products for our customers. He brought in one of his original paintings to show us. It was a commission piece, and he was going to deliver it to his customer that day. The large canvas he held was covered with abstract, psychedelic shapes. It wasn't something I usually cared for, but the colors and free expressive strokes were so artistic. I told him I liked all the movement and color combinations, and he said, "Yeah, I was really feeling good when I did this one," and laughed. "Had fun, and I'm going to get paid for it too. Right on, man!" he remarked as he walked away, whistling with his canvas.

I stayed away from Cade as most of us did. I only talked to him when I was forced to. I didn't care for his narrow, bigoted thinking and didn't want to know him any better. If we never spoke again, that would be fine with me. All that came out of his mouth was hateful, racist remarks. Other men worked in technical, but we hadn't met, and I hadn't learned their names yet or what they might be like.

The twins down in the photo lab amused me. They were identical twins and looked like carbon copies with their blond, curly hair and blue eyes. It was so difficult to tell them apart. They even finished each other's sentences. I thought it was odd that both had been hired to work the same job. I found out one of the twins had been hired a year earlier. When his coworker left for another job, he suggested his brother be hired to fill that spot since he was familiar with photo lab work. They worked hard down there, doing all the slides and overhead projections and photographing and resizing art, galleys, line drawings, and pictures for all the departments. They were like mushrooms thriving in the dark. When there was photographing to do, the white lights flashed and then they sloshed paper and chemicals under red lights. All of that was done in the damp, enclosed area of the photographic darkroom.

The owner of AdArt&Tech was Mr. Stevens. He was always entertaining new customers and promoting his business. I had never been in his large downstairs office but heard from Dean it was very comfortable with tufted leather chairs, a shag carpet, and a full bar. Mr. Stevens always wore the finest suits, shirts, and ties. A large gold ring with a big, red gemstone surrounded by diamonds was prominent on his finger. He also wore an expensive watch and a heavy gold chain bracelet. He wasn't a large man, and with his dark hair and complexion, I assumed he had a Hispanic background. He had a presence of importance you felt when you saw him. You knew he was the head of the company, and we all sat up and paid attention when he came upstairs. Fortunately, that wasn't too often. Usually, we only saw him when he was wooing a new client to the agency and showing off the different departments and our capabilities.

Our receptionist was pleasant and often said things that made us laugh. She was from Little Rock, Arkansas. She had quite a southern accent with a twang. It worked to her benefit because people listened carefully to the way she spoke and pronounced everything. She was friendly, outgoing, and efficient. Most of the time, she kept busy answering the phone and screening calls to the other departments or greeting customers. She also did steno work for Mr. Stevens or typed correspondence. She was young and married, but I didn't know much more about her. We'd say hello in the break room while getting a snack, but we were both so busy we never had the chance to talk except for a few words in greeting.

I didn't see the people from billing who worked downstairs often either. They were secreted away some place on the first floor and our paths seldom crossed. I didn't even know how many people worked in that department. Occasionally, one of them would come upstairs to ask about the numbers written on our daily timesheets. They were all filled out by hand, and we were told to do that in pencil.

We had to write down the name of the customer, their job number, and then our start and stop times. Sometimes billing had trouble reading an employee's handwriting. We didn't punch a time clock. With entries written in pencil, they could pad the times spent on a job by altering the entries. I knew that was being done for a lot of the government work.

More than once I had to do personal work for a coworker and put the time on a government job I was doing. Our receptionist had me put together a newspaper ad for her husband's new cleaning business, and Dean had me do a poster for a golf tournament for his club. Dean told me to write the time in on the government job. Billing the government for other people's work was normal there. I didn't like doing it but didn't know how to say no. Lyla and Maria often typed up personal business copy and brochures for coworkers too. Working on a "government job" became a joke that we all knew and understood. I talked to Samuel about that problem and asked if people did personal work on his job too.

"It sort of sticks out if you have a car in a truck repair shop, hon," he said. "Our boss will let the guys bring their cars in on their lunchtime to change the oil or something quick like that, but they can't charge anyone for parts or time working on their own vehicles."

"I don't feel comfortable doing personal work for others and charging it to the government," I told him. "It's really like stealing the taxpayers' money, don't you think?"

"Yeah, but if that's the norm there, then that's what you go with. Especially if your department boss is asking you to do something like that. You're new there, Josey, and if you complain, you'll be the first one to lose your job. Not someone else. Whistleblowers seldom get rewarded. They usually get the shaft instead," Samuel told me.

"God, I hate making these kinds of compromises," I said, but he was right. I shouldn't get the ones in power angry with me.

Dean, Lyla, Maria, and I still went out to lunch a couple of times a week to a restaurant nearby. It was at one of those lunches that someone brought up the subject of the upcoming election. I told them I liked the things I heard and saw Robert Kennedy do. He was running for the Democratic Party.

Lyla said, "I like Richard Nixon. He's the candidate for the Republican Party, and he's running a strong race as well."

Maria said, "Kennedy sounds good, but he's a Democrat like Johnson who hasn't ended the war. Richard Nixon said he could get us out of Vietnam and bring our troops home with peace and honor. Did you notice Nixon smiles a lot? I like that. His wife, Pat, seems like a strong, confident woman. She would make a good first lady. Nixon says he speaks for the silent majority who want our streets to be safe once more, and he said he could bring our country together."

Dean added, shaking his head, "And then there's Governor George Wallace from Alabama. He's running for president too. I guess he has a lot of backing in the southern states because of his segregation views, and he'll win those electoral votes, but he doesn't expect to win the election. He believes Nixon and Kennedy will have a close race and win about equal electoral votes. He's hoping to take enough Electoral College votes from the other two, so there's no definite winner. Then deciding the election would go to the House of Representatives. He believes he might have some power to persuade the House to determine he was the winner."

Lyla suddenly had an idea. "Let's have a mock debate," she said. "Maria, you can be Nixon, I'll be Kennedy, and Dean, you can be Wallace."

"Well, you'd be a good Kennedy," Dean said. "You talk funny like him."

"I talk funny!" Lyla said, offended. "I speak proper British English; it's you bloody Americans who murder the language. Come on, Dean, let's have a debate," she begged. "It'll be fun. Maria, are you in?"

"No, I'd rather not talk about the war and all," she answered, looking away.

"Josey, do you want to be Nixon?" Lyla asked, turning to me.

"I don't know a lot about his views, Lyla. Why don't you and Dean have a go at it? That could be interesting since Wallace and Kennedy are polar opposites," I told her.

"Why do I have to be George Wallace?" Dean asked. "You know I don't think like him."

"Because you're a red-blooded man with pants and all that goes in them, and you probably can understand how a blue-collar worker would think better than us fragile, empty-headed ladies," Lyla said sarcastically, batting her eyelashes. "Come on, use your male, superior brain to help us understand the middle-class workers who are hooked on Wallace and his American Independent Party."

"Okay, okay," Dean said as he gave in to her pleading. "But I'm not pulling any punches, you hear me, Kennedy?"

Lyla answered, "Right, and now Governor Wallace, why did you stand in the schoolhouse door in Alabama to stop a black student from entering? You were defying a federal law to integrate all the schools."

Dean as Wallace told her, "I say to that, Segregation now! Segregation tomorrow! Segregation forever! I came from the heart of the Confederacy, and no one's going to tell me what to do, especially the damn Yankee government with all its bureaucratic laws and court decisions!" Dean answered, shaking his finger at us and trying to put some Southern into his accent. "Now I have a question for you, Mr. Robert Kennedy of Hee-anus-port, Massachusetts. Just what are you going to do about all these damn hippies with their long hair and peace signs protesting the war in our cities? They should all be locked up and prosecuted."

Lyla, as Kennedy answered, "It's every American's right to speak his views publicly and work for change. Remember the First Amendment, Mr. Wallace, or do you feel that law should be ignored too?"

Dean puffed himself up. "Those people, those radicals on the college campuses, those preaching from the pulpits, the newspaper people, and those damn bureaucrats are all looking down their noses at us, the average man. Hell, young men are burning the American flag and their draft cards in public, making a show of it. It's shameful. It's disgusting. They're our enemies, I tell you—the militants, the students, the liberals, the newspapers, all of them are our enemies!" Dean was getting all fired up, sounding just like Governor Wallace, waving his arms and shaking his head, and was very convincing. "It's us against them," he added.

Lyla asked him, "Well, how would you go about changing laws and practices you thought were unfair if you were one of those student protestors, Governor Wallace?" She was doing good, trying to sound like Kennedy.

"I sure wouldn't do what those damn free love hippies are doing. Let them try burning our Southern flag. They'll find out what a southern barbeque is, I'll bet! And do you know those bureaucrats want to tell you who you have to rent or sell your house to? That just ain't right. I'm not going to let that happen. I'm going to clean out Washington and get rid of all those goddamn liberals."

Lyla replied, "Mr. Wallace, I believe any man, regardless of race or color or their position in life should have a chance to better themselves. They should be able to live where they want. Children of any race should be able to attend good schools with up-to-date books and teaching materials."

"Well, if you let them coloreds into our schools, next thing is, they'll be wanting to move onto your block. How are you gonna like that, Mr. Bleeding Heart Liberal, having them live right next to you?" Dean asked, mocking Lyla as Kennedy.

"I wouldn't mind that at all, Mr. Wallace. I've met some really fine black men and women who are hard-working Christian people, and if it takes Civil Rights busing or passing laws to bring fairness and balance to our schools so all the children can have equal opportunities, I say let's give it a try," Lyla added as Kennedy. "What do you think?"

"There's where you are wrong, Mr. Robert Kennedy from Hee-anus-port," Dean said. "The government wants to tell me where my kids have to go to school. They're going to snatch our kids out of their neighborhoods and send them way across town to some black ghetto school full of crime. That just ain't right!" Dean/Wallace added emphatically.

Then Lyla/Kennedy said, "I intend to help the poor people, Mr. Wallace, and make sure little children don't have empty bellies. Sometimes people just need a hand up. What would you do for them? Anything at all?"

"Damn bunch of freeloaders. Let 'em get a job and pay their own damn way. Those people are just lazy, I say, lazy, that's all. And I'll stop foreign aid too. That's just like dumping money down a rat hole," Dean/Wallace said.

"Wow, Dean, you make a great Wallace," Lyla said.

Maria and I applauded their performances, and they both took a bow. Then Maria looked at her watch and told us, "Oh, oh, we have to get back to work." We paid our bill and left. I had listened to the mock debate closely and asked Dean if what he had said as Wallace was true.

"Does he honestly believe we should still have segregation over one hundred years since the Civil War?"

"Yes, he does, Josey. I've been reading about his actions and the statements he's made. The scary part is that many people are listening to him. They think he's some sort of savior for the United States. They'll probably vote for his American Independent Party ticket. He's going to take votes away from Kennedy and Nixon and split those parties. He always talks about the things he's 'fed up' with, and he's just repeating the complaints of many others. His campaign slogan is 'Stand up for America,' and who doesn't want to do that? He's manipulating them. He's playing on people's fears and using the patriotism they have for our country to his benefit. He's even using their religious beliefs to get their votes even though a man like that certainly can't be following the Bible's teachings of 'love one another.' Now, I must go brush my teeth. I've got a bad taste in my mouth from repeating his words!" Dean said, shaking his head.

# Chapter 7

Eli and Hope were becoming good friends. Hope was a gentle, respectful woman who stayed home to care for her two daughters because her husband worked long hours. She was a good homemaker and enjoyed her job caring for their girls, keeping house, and cooking delicious meals for them. Eli made a decent salary, so Hope did not need or want to work.

Although she wasn't Amish, she often shared yummy Amish food with us. We would hear a knock at the door, and one of her daughters would deliver a jar of chow-chow or a pan of Amish breakfast casserole to us. Another time, we got some Shoofly pie, a delicious molasses dessert. I was washing a jar that had held some of her chicken corn soup. I dried it off and asked my son, Lucas, to take the jar across the hall to her.

"Now, be sure and hand it right back to Hope, then say, 'thank you very much. We really liked it,'" I instructed him. Lucas was younger than our daughter, but I thought it was an easy task for him to do. The kids went back and forth between our apartments to play all the time. He went out the door to deliver it, and I watched through the peephole to make sure he was at their door before I went to finish up the dishes. He returned a few minutes later, and I asked him if he had handed her the jar and remembered to say, "thank you very much. We loved the soup."

He said, "Yes, Mommy, I did," and went back to his room. About ten minutes later, there was a knock on my door. I opened it to see Hope standing there in her bathrobe. She had a towel wrapped around her hair and a serious look on her face.

"Did Lucas say anything to you when he came back?" she asked.

"No. Why? Is something wrong?"

Then she started laughing as she told me what had happened. She said Lucas knocked on the apartment door, and she had called back, "I'm busy right now." She had left the bathroom door ajar slightly to listen for her daughters, and before she knew what was happening, Lucas was beside her in the bathroom, where she was stark naked, taking a bath. She quickly tried to hide under the bubbles while Lucas handed her the jar and said, "Mommy told me to say thank you."

"Oh my God, Hope, I didn't know he would do something like that. I'm so sorry. I've never let him see me naked like that or come into the bathroom when I'm using it," I said, covering my mouth and grimacing.

Hope patted my arm. "It's all right, Josey. My girls let him in, and it was a perfectly innocent mistake. I thought you would like to know, just in case he told you I was running around naked in my apartment." She was laughing loudly now, and I started laughing right along with her.

"It must have been comical to see me scrambling to cover up with those bubbles. I hope he completely forgets the flash of flesh he saw. I don't want to get blackmailed by your little guy," she said teasingly, and we started laughing all over again. We had to wipe tears from our eyes before we hugged and said goodbye. She was such a good friend.

Hope and I often lounged in the reclining chairs by the pool together and soaked up the warm Maryland sun while our children splashed about in the water under the careful watch of the lifeguard. It was tanning and relaxing while the lifeguard helped you monitor your kids for free. Samuel and I only went out occasionally because of our different schedules. Hope and Eli did not go out much either because he worked over sixty hours a week most of the time. He wanted to stay home and relax with his family when he had time off.

I could tell Hope did not care much for living in DC. She spoke wistfully of living in Lancaster and the tasty food you could get there. She missed buying smoked sharp cheese cut right off a block and getting slices of sweet Lebanon bologna. She enjoyed eating rosy pickled eggs and having sandwiches made on homemade Amish sourdough bread. Hope missed seeing the Amish in their buggies on the road, even though they held up traffic with their horse-drawn carriages. Mostly, she missed the farmlands with their crops of corn and wheat and the open spaces of the countryside and beautiful old farms.

I asked her, "You get a lot of snow in Lancaster, don't you? Like we did where we lived up north? I'm so glad to be out of it right now. Winters there can be so long and bitter cold. Did you go outside much in winter, Hope?"

"No, I pretty much stayed inside most of the time," she answered.

Then I told her, "I don't do winter sports like skiing or ice fishing. It gets depressing for me to be shut up inside, and I hate driving on icy, slippery roads. Often the snow is so deep you can't even walk around your own yard. You have to follow a narrow path you shoveled just to get to your car or in and out of the house."

Hope replied, "We did get some heavy snows where we lived. But sometimes it's like taking a vacation from all the activities of warmer weather. Winter slows everything down. There are so many activities and things we must do outdoors when the weather is nice. We have to mow the lawn and take care of the vegetable garden and weed. We take a lot of trips in summer too and visit relatives. It seems like we're constantly in the car to some sports game or parties for someone. Winter can be so peaceful and beautiful when the snow falls and covers everything with a fresh white blanket like it's tucking things in until springtime. It's a beautiful new landscape."

"I know what you mean, Hope. Everything looks so different . . . so clean and new."

Hope continued, "I like it too when I have time to do a lot of reading, and baking, and playing board games with the kids. Just hanging out watching a video or reading to them is enjoyable. I knit scarves and mittens for them. I do some quilting, and we relax and spend hours together.

When we do go outdoors, we might go sledding or build a snowman. I'm like a kid playing with them. Once, we even built a snow turtle. The kids had fun sitting on it and pretending they were going somewhere at a very slow pace. Often, after being outside for a while, we would come back in with rosy cheeks and cold fingers and have hot chocolate with marshmallows in it. I love the smell and warmth of the woodstove and tunneling down under a warm quilt. We had good times, even in snowy weather," she said wistfully.

"There are a few things I like about winter too. Have you ever seen a hoar frost in the morning when the sun makes ice crystals on the grass, bushes, and trees that sparkle like brilliant diamonds in the sun? It is almost like someone dipped all the trees in white glitter overnight. Every single tiny twig and branch sparkles. It's just awesome! When the sun is bright and it casts shadows on the snow, they can be such an intense blue. I like seeing how the wind can sculpt the snow into drifts. Sometimes they look like white ocean waves curling over on the top, ready to hit the beach of the road."

"Yes, but that road can be pretty darn slippery!" Hope commented.

I told her, "I had fun with the kids too, building snowmen and a snow horse—with no legs of course. One time, we even made a snow dinosaur. We used packages of green Kool-Aid to add color to it. We've made snow ice cream with vanilla stirred into a batch of fresh snow. It doesn't taste anything like real ice cream, but it's fun for the kids to pretend."

"The kids don't mind winter at all," Hope said. "They think it's a great time to play."

I told her, "Icicles can make a house look like a fancy decorated cake when they hang from the eaves. You can always tell it has snowed a lot when those icicles grow so long they hang halfway down the outside wall. When I was young, my sister and I would break them off, sprinkle some salt on them, and crunch on that hard ice like it was a frozen crystal carrot."

"Ouch, that sounds like it was hard on your teeth!" Hope said.

"Yes, kind of hard on the teeth," I told her. "But the worst part was the brain freeze you got from eating that ice too fast. Those were good family times, I remember. As an adult, though, I still don't like scraping ice off my windshield and driving on dangerous roads when they aren't plowed off and sanded well. It's too hard to go out someplace like work or get groceries in winter. We lived on a steep hill, and more than once, my car slid into a ditch. One time my car stopped going uphill because the road was so slippery. Instead, it was sliding down the hill backward. God, that was scary! I wiped out a neighbor's mailbox that day," I told her. "I'm enjoying this warm Maryland weather a lot more."

Then I continued. "Talking about winter back home reminds me of something that happened up there. The water from the road in front of our house would run down our long driveway and freeze into sheets of ice. I often had to park up at the road, since it was so slippery and diffi-cult to get traction to drive the car up and down it. My boss had given us all a nice bottle of wine on the Friday before Christmas break. I was looking forward to opening it and celebrating the holiday with Samuel. That afternoon I got out of the car up at the top of the driveway with the wine in one hand and my purse in the other. I carefully started walking down the icy driveway when my feet suddenly went out from under me, and with a whoosh, then slam, I was lying face up on my back, looking at the clouds."

"Oh, no!" Hope said, then asked, "Did you get hurt?"

"Well, I lay there for a few moments. I had the wind knocked out of me, and I was starting to feel some possible bruising and soreness, but luckily nothing felt broken. I had saved that bottle of wine by raising my arm when I fell, so that didn't get broken, either. I lay there, trying to fig-ure out how to stand back up on that ice when I heard a familiar noise. It was the school bus dropping a neighbor's kids off further down the road, and it was now headed my way." I asked Hope, "Can you imagine what a sight our neighbor's children would have seen looking out the school bus window when it passed our place? I would have looked like a drunk mom who passed out in the driveway in the afternoon!"

"What did you do?" Hope asked.

"I got up as fast and safely as I could and turned to face the bus before it got to my driveway. My whole backside was white with snow. I hid the bottle of wine behind my back and smiled and waved at the driver and the students. Then, after it pulled away, I crept over to where the snow was on the grass. 'Don't go near that ice again,' I told myself. Boy, did that wine taste good later when I parked my sore fanny on a heating pad!" Hope and I were laughing so hard when my story ended, we had to wipe tears from our eyes again.

We were quiet for a few moments after that. Then Hope added, "I think what I miss most right now is the peace and the open space. Here it's noisy all the time and the sky is small, and I can't even see the stars at night. There are so many lights shining my eyes can't focus and see past them. I miss looking up and seeing the Big Dipper and the other stars shining in the dark sky. The neighbors I had in Lancaster were just hardworking people living simple lives in the country and we weren't living in an apartment. We had a yard, and I had a flower garden. I'm not used to having people right on top of me like this all the time. People are living over us and beside us. When we go out here, we're surrounded by so many people and cars on the road. Anyplace we go, we're in a crowd. There's no privacy, no breathing space. I feel bookended and sandwiched all the time."

"I know what you mean. I hear every step my neighbors take in the apartment above me. Do you know what the woman upstairs did the other day?"

"What happened now?" Hope asked.

"She let her daughter roller skate back and forth above us for hours. Or, it could have been her on roller skates. It sounded that heavy and loud. Can you imagine what that noise was like downstairs in my place? Do you know what else my upstairs neighbor did? She stepped out on her balcony the other day and shook her rugs over us while we were sitting right beneath on our patio. We were just quietly soaking in the sunshine, and suddenly dust and dirt rained down on us. It made us choke, and I yelled at her to stop. I usually like everyone, but she's so inconsiderate! She never even checked to see if someone was sitting beneath her balcony."

"I know what you mean about the noise bothering you," Hope said. "The couple above us fight and slam doors. They must throw things around, too, because I hear crashing noises. The fights don't last long, but the language they use, it's terrible. I'm glad the girls usually sleep soundly, so they don't hear that language."

Hope seldom used any kind of swear word, so I knew how much that could upset her. She was a genuinely gentle person, and I felt comfortable and blessed to have her as my friend. We enjoyed each other's company and talked about dreams for our kids and just about everything else going on. "I'll bet some of these people just love all this closeness and constant contact with others and activity, though. They probably would be scared to death or bored and lonely with all the peace and quiet of the countryside we love." We sat quietly for a few minutes, lost in our thoughts and memories as we watched the children splash about.

"Have you checked out the elementary school yet?" Hope asked. "Grace is starting school soon. There's an open house orientation for parents coming up. The school has two sessions. Why don't I keep Grace and Lucas while you and Samuel go to the school? Afterward, you can watch ours. Then Eli and I can go to the second session." It sounded like a good plan, so we agreed to do that.

Hope and I often chatted about the different lives and responsibilities women have these days and how we felt about the Women's Liberation Movement going on. The swimming lesson was almost over when one of the mothers walked by us. Hope and I couldn't help but notice she was a shapely woman wearing a snug white T-shirt without a bra. After she walked past us, Hope and I turned to each other, raised our eyebrows, and grinned.

"She must be one of those woman libbers," Hope said.

"Yes," I answered, "she liberated the girls for sure. Did you see the television coverage of some of those women wanting to be 'liberated?' A bunch of them were burning their bras at the Miss America Pageant in Atlantic City. It showed them tossing their underwear into the fire."

"They did?" Hope answered. "Darn, I missed that."

"Cronkite covered it. They were dumping bras and girdles, high heels and makeup into a big burn barrel and setting them on fire," I told her. "They said they weren't going to shave their legs or armpits anymore either."

"I don't think I could ever go braless in public," Hope said.

"I don't think I could either. Bras aren't just to cover us up, they're for support. By the time those women are forty, those girls will be pointing at the floor. They'll be sorry they let it all hang out," I told her, laughing.

"What would the Amish men in Lancaster say about women wearing T-shirts with no bra?"

"They would say, 'Those English to hell are going soon!' It's a male-run religious society. The women must obey their husbands and the male elders in their church," she said. "There is another saying the men have. *'Sooner would I single live than to my wife the britches give.'* I'm all for improving women's lives and some of the issues women are talking about these days, though," Hope said and added, "You know what I don't understand? Those libbers want men to see them as intelligent people and not just as sexy bodies. Well, isn't going without a bra and wearing a tight T-shirt ruining that? Their breasts are jiggling away, and their nipples are so obvious, it's doing just the opposite. No man will be looking at her face or listening closely to what she's saying. He isn't thinking about how smart she is with all that activity going on."

"You've got a point there, Hope," I said, "or is that two points?" and we started laughing so hard we had tears flowing once again.

Then I added, "Well, there's another thing the feminists want to change. No more shaving legs or armpits, either. I hate shaving my legs, but I hated seeing that black hair growing on them like an ape even more. The first time I shaved them was in the shower. I soaped up my leg, pressed on that brand-new sharp razor, and shaved from my ankle to my knee. I looked at the razor, and it had a long, narrow ribbon of my skin hanging from it. Then I looked down at my leg to see blood streaming and red soapy bubbles going down the drain. Boy, that stung!"

"Yikes!" Hope said. "I'll bet it did. There was a woman on television the other day who raised her arm, and it looked like a bird's nest in her armpit. Makes me itch just thinking about it."

"Yeah, I think they're going too far. I don't think women should be accepted as equals because we dress, act, or groom ourselves like a man. We should have equal pay and rights because we deserve it and work as hard as a man on our jobs, often even harder."

"I agree," Hope said. "And don't get me started on what a mother and a homemaker should be paid."

"What do you think about an Amish woman's life?" I asked Hope. "It seems to me that it's such a small world for them, such an isolated and limited life. I mean, how far from home can you go with a horse and buggy? There's so much they aren't allowed to do. They aren't allowed to watch television to see what's going on in the rest of the world. I'm not sure if they can read any novel they want, and they certainly cannot go to the movies. They cannot wear makeup or jewelry or even cut their hair short. Everything they do has to follow strict rules the men of the church outline for them. The girls have to quit school at age fourteen. What bothers me too is that they must always work so hard. It seems unfair that they're forced to give up so much."

"But are they giving up something they never had to miss?" Hope asked. "I mean, how can you really miss something when you don't even know what you're missing? They might like having rules for how to dress and act. They know exactly what's expected of them and don't have to spend a lot of time picking out clothes or shopping for an outfit. That's fun for us, but they might enjoy getting fabric and sewing their own outfits that fit what's allowed. I know sometimes they buy or barter clothes from another Amish woman who is a seamstress. Their children always seemed so happy when I saw them playing outdoors. It's hard to understand how those women can accept a life that seems so limited to us. Some are craftspeople and quilters and make things to sell or they bake goods for farmer's markets. I don't think their life isn't full. I just think their world is smaller than ours but not necessarily worse."

Hope continued, "We have so many choices. Sometimes, I think too many. Their life is definitely not so complex or worldly. There's something admiral about living a simple, ordered life that brings them happiness. Look at how they support and help each other with everything from building a new barn to caring for the sick. They can always count on a neighbor to be there when help is needed. They share and barter everything. Maybe the rest of us should follow some of their examples. The women and men work so hard in this life, because they believe heaven will be more rewarding for them. So, they do it. Perhaps a simple, dedicated family life can be more of a blessing to some than one full of television, or careers, or politics. Look at how some monks live, yet they feel fulfilled and at peace."

I thought about what Hope said and told her, "Down here in Maryland and DC, everybody is doing their own thing for themselves. Most of these people don't know who's living right beside them, let alone knowing if someone needs help or not. I guess we'll never know what Amish life is truly like. We cannot understand how they live or what they believe unless we've been raised that way. What is that saying? You have to walk in someone else's shoes? I just could not be happy with a man telling me what I could or could not do for everything in my life. I prefer having a discussion and making decisions together. I think God gave us brains and free will for some reason. Maybe it was to choose what we wanted our own life to be and not live by the limits others may put on us. I could not live without a good novel or watching Ed Sullivan on Sunday night. Oh, and a glass of wine now and then. God bless those Amish women, though, for what they do for their families. Sometimes I wonder if I should be living a simpler life, especially when I'm stuck in the horrible traffic down here and the pressures I have at work! It's really hard to be a mother and have a career too."

Then I told her, "We took a trip to Lancaster one weekend a couple of years ago and saw a small group of Amish women standing together talking in front of a store. I told my children, 'Look how neat and clean those ladies are. Their clothes are so nicely pressed, and they have those pretty white bonnets on their hair.' Just then, one of them turned her head and spat nasty brown tobacco juice onto the ground. Then she wiped her mouth with the back of her hand. I had to laugh because seeing her chewing on that stuff seemed so out of character."

Another day, Hope and I were sipping our morning coffee together on my patio, enjoying the start of our day as our children played together. Soon our oldest girls would be going to school for the first time. We were both quiet for a few moments, then Hope spoke up and asked me, "Josey, do you ever think about what you want your children to learn in their lives?"

"I've thought a lot about that," I told her. "I want my children to know deep love and kindness. They should know what it feels like to win and how to handle losing and realize it's an opportunity to be humble and find the lesson in it if they do. Then it isn't a loss—it's a gain. I want them to be proud of their effort even if it doesn't get the result they wanted. They need to be respectful of others and reverent and believe in God. I hope they learn not to be afraid of trying new things, to take adventures, to be joyful and seek happiness above money or status. How about you, Hope? What would you like your children to learn?"

"I want them to feel compassion for those that suffer and are disadvantaged in life and try to help them. I want them to know they have the genes of strength and stamina from their ancestors who survived the most difficult of times in their blood and they can rise above whatever challenges they face. I want them to know how to be happy and find contentment and blessings in their lives and be grateful for everything. Not just for the gifts they're given but for the challenges that test them and those that make them wiser and stronger," Hope said.

"I'm hoping ours learn all that too, Hope," I said. "I'm counting on mine to keep seeking knowledge and truth and learn. I want them to open their eyes to nature and experience spending time in it to learn its beauty and the rhythm of the seasons. I'm hoping they learn that others have different lives than theirs and experiences that shape them. They should help others when they can. I hope they learn to avoid negative people and people with low standards or values and choose good friends and partners."

I continued, "Most of all, I hope they don't postpone joy and happiness. Samuel and I are always saying, 'when we get more money, we'll go on a great vacation.' But that's always so far out of our reach, way off into the future. My parents never did anything except work every day. They never really retired, and before they knew it, the years had gone by, and they were seniors with health problems and a limited income. By then it was impossible to go to the places they had dreamed about decades ago. I hope our children learn to set happiness goals and reach them before it's too late." We both sat silently, sipping our coffee and thinking of our children and their futures for some time that morning.

A couple of weeks later, we toured the classrooms at Bladensburg Elementary and spoke with the kindergarten teacher. The red brick building was old but clean. It was the end of the school year, and the kindergartners would soon be coming for a half-day visit. They would meet the teachers they would have in September. First, though, the school wanted to prepare the parents for that day. On the day of the parents' orientation, Samuel and I perched on short, little chairs around the low wood tables and listened to the kindergarten teacher. We were given handouts of required medical shots and brief talks about making sure our young ones got into a regular sleep schedule before next September. They also needed to be taught their full name and phone number and be able to count to ten.

"We will teach them how to print, not you, please," she said. "It's hard to undo something you have shown them wrong, and for God's sake, make sure they can go to the bathroom by themselves and don't need someone to wipe their little butt! I haven't got time for that with twenty-five to thirty students."

Samuel leaned over and whispered, "Boy, she gets right to the important stuff, doesn't she? Or should I say right to the butt of the matter?"

"Shh . . . Listen, Samuel, this is important," I told him.

The teacher did not seem as nurturing and motherly as I had hoped. However, she gave me confidence that she was in control of things. Looking around the room at the colorful artwork and posters, it felt like what a school should be.

There was a multiracial mix of parents in the room. It would be good for Grace to experience what the rest of the world is like. It was so different from the white bread world Samuel and I had been raised in. It made us feel better that she would be in the same classroom as Hope's daughter.

The teacher continued with her directions. "And don't get all emotional and go to the end of the hallway when you drop your child off for their short visit and start blubbering away 'My baby, my baby,'" she said. "It just upsets them. You need to get out of the building fast. Do not go to a window to look in, either. They will be okay. Even if they start crying, they will stop after a short while if you just disappear."

I knew it would be hard, though, to trust a bus driver and strange teacher to care for our precious little girls.

* * *

Hope and I waited anxiously together when the first school day came in September. There was a large group of mothers waiting with us in the corner of our apartment's parking lot. We kept our emotions under control until the bus pulled away, then Hope and I looked at each other and laughed because we were both crying. Our babies would now be handed over to another person for hours. We would miss some funny things they said and did. Someone else would be giving them life lessons. We wouldn't be able to see them, and if they were scared, or needed help, we would not be there to comfort them. It was tough. We didn't realize it then, but later we got used to the routine and looked forward to some quiet, free time to ourselves.

The days did get a rhythm to them around the pickup and delivery of our little students. After a while, the mothers at the apartments decided there was no reason a large group of us had to meet the bus each day. They worked out a plan for rotating pairs of moms and dads to meet the bus. They would escort the kids to their apartments in a group. So, we all had a schedule and took turns doing that job.

Life was going along smoothly with our work and the kids in school until just before Christmas. Something happened to Hope. Samuel had left for his night job at the shop. Hope asked me to watch her girls for a short while. She wanted to pick up some items for a special supper she was making for her and Eli and would only be gone for a short time. The store was just a few blocks away. When it was getting dark and she hadn't returned, I decided to feed all the children.

Her little girl was concerned and said, "Mommy said she would be right back, and we would have a special supper."

"I know, sweetie, but she probably had to get more groceries than she thought. Maybe she couldn't find what she needed and had to go to another store. She'll be here soon," I assured her, although I was getting worried too.

After more than four hours, I heard a light knock on my door. I opened it to see Hope standing there looking terrible. Her hair was wet like she had taken a shower, and you could tell she had been crying a lot. As soon as she saw me, she started crying again. The kids were all playing together in a back bedroom. I heard a voice call out, "Is that my mommy?" from one of her daughters.

I yelled back. "Yes, but we want to talk a bit, hon. Keep playing for now, okay?" Then I turned back to Hope and asked in a concerned voice,

"Hope, what's the matter? What happened to you? I was getting worried. I fed the children."

"I'm so ashamed," she blurted out. "I've been in my apartment. I had to take a shower."

I looked at her closer and noticed she had bruises on her arms. I immediately reached out and hugged her, and she winced. "Oh my God, Hope . . . what's going on? Did you have an accident? Are you hurt? I see bruises, and why are you so upset?"

"No, it's not an accident," she said, then paused, "It's worse!" She buried her face in her hands and sobbed. Then she took a deep breath and started talking to me.

"I was walking to my car with my bag of groceries. It was parked right next to a white van in the back corner of the parking lot. I stepped between the van and my car to put the groceries in the back seat. Just when I leaned in, a man grabbed me from behind. He covered my mouth with his hand so I couldn't scream. There was no one else around. He opened the back door of the van, forced me inside, and shut the door. It didn't have any windows in the back, and no one could see what he did to me. Oh, God!" she said and broke down sobbing hard again.

"Oh no, Hope, what did he do?" I asked her with my arms around her. "Did he hurt you? How did you get away? Are you all right?"

"He raped me, Josey," she said. "I couldn't fight him off. He was too strong. I'm so ashamed. When he was done with me, he just laughed, then he jumped out of the van and took off running. He just left me lying there on the floor of the van. It wasn't even his van. When I saw he was gone, I crawled out of the van and drove home. I had to take a shower. I had to get clean. Oh, what am I going to do, Josey? What time is it? It must be late. Eli will be home anytime." And she buried her face in her hands, sobbing again.

"Hope, you need to call the police. You need to tell them what happened and go to the hospital. They've got to catch this guy."

"No, no, I can't do that," she said. "I am so ashamed. I can't talk about it to strangers. They'll ask me all kinds of questions. I'm so embarrassed—I feel so dirty. Why did he pick me? What did I do?" She was still sobbing hard as I tried to comfort her and figure out how I could help.

"Did you get a good look at his face? I can help you report this, Hope."

"Yes, he was a white man, about thirty years old. I never thought . . . and it was daytime . . ." Her voice trailed off.

"I can call the police for you, and I'll stay by your side."

"No, I don't want anyone to find out. It would be in the newspapers and probably on television. I don't want the neighbors or my children to find out and ask questions. What would I say to my girls? They're just little children. I can't face my neighbors if they know what . . . ." Her voice trailed off again.

"Hope, listen to me. This is not your fault. You are a victim of a crime. You've got to tell Eli as soon as you can. He can help you go to the police," I told her gently, holding her shoulders and looking into her tear-filled eyes. "Why don't we let your girls have a sleepover here tonight? You can be alone with Eli while you work out what to do. If you don't report this, that lowlife will hurt another woman. Are you sure you don't need a doctor, a policewoman, or someone else to talk to?"

"I can't, Josey, I can't," Hope said as she lowered her head and shook it back and forth. "All the questions they would ask and how they treat a woman who has been attacked . . . They always make it sound like she asked for it, like she teased him and led him on. There might be an arrest and then newspaper coverage and a trial. I would have to testify. I'd have to see him again. I can't, I just can't," she kept saying. "Eli will be home soon. I do have to tell him, and he'll be so angry. I don't want to be here anymore. I'll never feel safe again. Oh, my little girls, my little girls, they aren't safe here either. We've got to leave. I have to keep them safe."

"Hope, don't make any of these decisions right now. I'll keep the girls for the night. You stay here with me until Eli comes home."

"I don't want the girls to see me so upset. I'm okay waiting in my apartment for him with the door locked. He'll be home anytime now." She sucked in a deep breath and straightened up. "I need to be alone with him to talk." She seemed calmer, more together now as she spoke.

"Okay, if you're sure. I'm right here across the hall if you change your mind and need me." We hugged again, and she felt so frail to me. I watched as she entered her apartment and shut the door. I hoped Eli would give her the courage to call the police.

I told her daughters that Mommy and Daddy needed some time alone, and they were fine with that. They were having such a fun time playing with my kids, and the idea of a sleepover with them, eating popcorn and watching a Disney movie, was exciting.

I couldn't help but think I could have been the woman attacked instead of Hope. I often shopped at the same store.

* * *

Hope and Eli picked up the girls the next morning. They told us they had decided to move back to Lancaster as soon as possible. I was shocked. They had chosen not to call the police and report what had happened. "We just want to put it all behind us," Eli said. "It'll be easier to forget what happened if we're somewhere Hope can feel safe again."

I encouraged them to report the attack, but their minds were made up. Eli had been a track star in school and said, "When you run up against a hurdle, you just jump over it and run on." He wasn't worried about leaving his job. Construction was picking up again, and he was going home to work with his brother, who had a business building houses in Lancaster. Eli had already called his boss and told them he was quitting. He told them his mother had become deathly ill, and he was sorry, but he needed to be near her while she fought for her life. Hope was terribly afraid of being left alone now. Eli didn't even want to leave her to go to his job for his belongings. She stayed with me, so he could leave. An assistant manager was going to take over his duties until they found his replacement. Eli may be able to run on after this terrible hurdle, but this one would be too large for Hope to just jump over and put behind her.

We shed so many tears those few days before we said our final goodbyes. Living in the apartment complex would not be the same without my good friend Hope. Our days of lying in the warm sun while our children splashed in the pool were over. But I knew she would feel safer back in Lancaster. I prayed she could heal there and become the happy, loving person I had known. I could not help but wonder how many other women had been attacked like Hope, wherever they lived, and never reported it.

## Chapter 8

Samuel and I had a heated discussion after Hope and Eli moved away. I told him we might have made a mistake moving to Maryland for his new job. Maybe it was not a good place to raise our children and we should think about moving back home, like Hope had. He got angry.

"Dammit, Josey!" he said. "Look at the great job I have. I can't leave it. You know how hard it was for us back home before we moved here. You have a decent job now, too. Why the hell would we leave all this when we're finally getting ahead?"

"Samuel, I'm concerned about living here. Are our children really safe? I'm worried for all of us," I told him.

"Why are you suddenly so afraid?" he asked. "Is it because of what happened to Hope? That was terrible and upsetting. My heart still breaks for her, but that doesn't mean something like that will happen to you, Josey. I'm right here with you whenever I can. Just be more cautious and aware of your surroundings—that's all."

"I don't think you realize what a different world a woman lives in than a man. Women and children are prey in this life. It should never be that way, but it is. You don't have to worry about who's leering at you or stalking you when you walk down a street or are out in public, do you? Does your heart ever quicken because you think someone might be following you or they may hurt you? I'll bet you never even think about something like that. And our children, it's horrible even to consider what terrible things might happen to them at the hands of someone else. We don't live in a world as safe as a man's world—your world, Samuel. It is a hugely different experience for women and children to live in this world." I was frustrated and teared up talking to him about how I felt. He didn't understand the big difference in our lives.

Seeing me so upset, Samuel wrapped his arms around me and said he was sorry he had gotten angry. He said he understood my fear after what Hope had gone through, but he felt we were in the place we should be living now, and everything was going to be all right for us. He told me to just hang in there and I would feel better soon.

As I had thought, living at the complex was not the same without my good friend Hope. Grace and Lucas missed playing with their girls, too. I tried to contact Hope after they had left, but she never returned my calls. I think they both wanted to cut off anything that might remind her of what had happened in the grocery store parking lot. After some time, I gave up trying to contact her and reluctantly moved on, too. As the weeks went on, I was cautiously vigilant watching over our children and only did my grocery shopping when Samuel was with me.

* * *

We already had a backlog of work with tight deadlines at the agency when the "big job" came in at AdArt&Tech. Everyone employed there had to get a top-secret clearance, which involved getting background checks, being photographed, fingerprinted, and interviewed personally by the FBI. I knew I had no reason I would not clear that investigation, but I wondered about some of my coworkers after going to Priscilla's cocktail party.

After the personal ID photos were taken and the security badges made, two FBI men fingerprinted us, one at a time. The next step was in-depth, personal interviews. I was alone in the conference room with two profoundly serious men who asked me so many prying questions.

They wrote down my answers on forms from a file folder with my name on its tab. Question after question was fired at me first by one agent and then the other.

"What are your parents' names? Where did they come from?" they asked. "Are they American citizens? Where do they live? What do they do for work? What are your brothers' and sisters' names? Who are they married to? Where do they live? What do they do for work? Who are your brother-in-law's parents? Your sister-in-law's parents? Where do they live? Are they American citizens? Where did they come from?"

I was so surprised at how far-reaching their search for information about my family was. I wondered if there might be something in my large family history that might become an obstacle to my clearance. After some time, I felt I might have committed a crime because the questioning was so intense. I even entertained the idea that I might need a lawyer. I also wondered about my coworkers' history and activities. Would they pass such a thorough inspection of their lives?

Two weeks later, we found out everyone had cleared the background checks. We were all gathered in the conference room when we got that news. We had to swear to an Oath of Secrecy regarding the document we would be working on. We listened intently as the FBI agent read the words to us. We raised our right hand and repeated, "I swear to a vow of Loyalty and Secrecy to the government of the United States, so help me God."

The agents warned us not to discuss the contents of the publication we were going to work on with anyone—not our spouses or even other coworkers. We were not allowed to make any copies, photographs, or drawings of the material. They said all scraps of paper trash would be collected by the FBI each day and destroyed. We were not allowed to write down any notes of what we were working on. No purses, briefcases, or lunch bags would be allowed in the room where we were working. All items had to be left outside our rooms with the FBI guard. One would be stationed at our doorways.

There was an air of excitement, wanting to know why we needed all this security. Only ten copies of the document would be made. One was for the President of the United States, and the others would be for the nine members of his cabinet. We knew it must be important for the government to go to so many steps and spend so much money for only ten copies. After the FBI men left the office that day, a conspiracy began that would weigh heavy on my heart for the rest of my life. I would forever be pulled in opposite directions, wondering if I had done the right thing.

As soon as the FBI men departed and we had returned to our departments, our boss announced all employees needed to return to the conference room. We quickly reassembled, expecting some sort of pep talk to get us fired up and welcome all the extra work involved with "the big job." Mr. Stevens seemed nervous for someone who had always seemed so confident. He began by saying, "You will all be making a lot of money with overtime, and there is no limit to what the agency can charge on this government job. Extra overtime is required to meet the ridiculous deadline the government has set, so we should all plan to work late for several nights when the copy arrives."

There was a happy gleam in his eyes as he rocked back and forth on his heels. "The agency is going to score big on this one, and if we put the push on, there will be a big bonus in it for you, too." He paused, then his face turned serious before he continued. "We have just one minor problem. I need your full cooperation on this for the good of the agency. Well, for the good of us all, actually." He paused again, put his hands on his hips, looked down at the floor, and drew in a deep breath. Then he spoke. "I need to have Lyla work on the typesetting. There is not enough time to train anyone else to do her job." He let us absorb those words for a minute. I did not understand what the problem was. Then he told us, "Lyla is considered an alien. She's from England and never got an American citizenship." He looked around, trying to read our faces as that statement soaked in, then said, "I did not tell the FBI she was on our payroll. If they find out, they will pull this top-secret job from us. We would be in trouble if that happened and never get another government job. You all know how much that would hurt our business. Think of how many jobs we do for the various agencies of the government. I need your cooperation on this matter. We have to keep it a secret that she will be working on this."

Looking around, I realized I had not seen Lyla in the group with us earlier. She was not there during the FBI fingerprinting or the interviews.

*How ironic,* I thought, *that we must keep it secret that an alien will be working on a top-secret publication.* Mr. Stevens told us he would give Lyla a key so she could enter the building before the rest of us and go right upstairs into the typesetting alcove. The FBI would not start checking badges downstairs until the rest of us came in at eight o'clock. Lyla would also leave the building by letting herself out after everyone left. The FBI had assured our boss that they would be posted outside our office doors to check badges for people coming and going from the building and would leave us alone in our departments the rest of the time to concentrate on our work. I realized no one would even see Lyla if they looked in our department door. The typesetting alcove has a wall that would block their view. Maria, Dave, Booker, and I looked at each other and raised our eyebrows. I wondered what each of them was thinking right then.

"Are you all with me on this?" Mr. Stevens asked, looking directly at everyone in the room but especially at the workers in my department. "I need to know that you'll keep Lyla's part a secret from the FBI men. They must not find out. Surely you all understand why and see how important it is. We will make a lot of money with this contract. We don't want to lose this job. I'm assuming everyone is okay with this?" He asked once again as he scanned the faces of his employees.

I looked around at my coworkers, and heads were nodding everywhere. Reluctantly, I nodded right along with them. How had they all agreed to such a serious security breach so quickly? Was this the normal way top-secret government work was handled? After Mr. Stevens realized his employees would go along with his deception, he smiled and said, "Great," then rubbed his hands together and dismissed us. I left the room with my coworkers, wondering what I had just committed to.

The next morning, an FBI man was stationed right inside the front door to our agency to check our badges as we entered the building. I fumbled to find mine in my purse when he asked me to show it to him. He told me firmly to wear that badge at all times so they would know I had been cleared. When I got upstairs, another FBI man was stationed in the hallway between the layout and technical departments. He told me to leave my purse with him and to please show him the contents of my pockets. I did, and he let me enter my work area. I heard him stop Cade at the technical department door because he had a little transistor radio in his shirt pocket. The guard said it might be a small tape recorder and took it from Cade. Two couriers delivered the top-secret copy a half hour later, and the work began.

We were not allowed to go out to lunch for the duration of the top-secret project. However, food could be delivered to us after our "guards" inspected it. Usually, I didn't read a lot of the copy on the pages I was working on. My job was to paste down galleys of type and fit in charts and diagrams like big puzzle pieces onto a page. I also needed to add headlines and figure captions under any photos. Often, I only glanced at the text as a block of type. Our proofreader, Priscilla, had the job of reading it all carefully while checking the originally submitted copy to make sure there were no grammar mistakes, data errors, or missing copy.

The paste-up for this job was quite different from our other work. Every page had "TOP SECRET" marked boldly in red capital letters on the top and bottom margins. It was impossible to miss that warning. I cringed when I saw those words, thinking about the deception. Maria and Lyla cranked out typesetting as fast as they could to keep the work flowing, and the technical department brought charts and drawings to us in a constant flow. I stepped into the typesetting alcove in our room to ask Maria a question. Lyla was working out of sight over in the corner. She had on the same badge the FBI had given us and fitted right in. I looked questioningly at her, and she lifted her badge and grinned at me. I didn't have to ask how she got it. We did typesetting and took photos all the time. It would have been easy to take her picture and make a duplicate of a real badge at the agency.

I turned away and walked back to my desk. I was even more troubled by the awful deception happening. It would be terrible if somehow the guard realized that Lyla had not gone through the clearance if he saw her. Besides that, we were all participating in such a grievous, disloyal, dishonest act against our own government. I had to push those guilty thoughts way back in my mind and concentrate on the work in front of me.

The day passed with us all working hard to keep the president's project moving. We gathered our belongings back from the FBI guard and left for the night—all except Lyla, hidden in the typesetting alcove. She would leave after everyone else had gone, especially the FBI guards.

The next morning, the guards checked badges again when we entered the building. Lyla had already snuck in. I resumed pasting up the galleys of type and the illustrations that were handed to me. I was also setting headlines for chapters, sections, and captions for the technical drawings. When the next diagram from technical came to me and I pasted it down, complete with its photo caption, I sucked in my breath and leaned back. Fear hit me when I realized how important this document was. Without thinking, I said, "Wow, I can't believe this!" way too loud. Dean had left the room, and thankfully, only Booker heard what I had said.

"Is something wrong with the copy? Technical screw up again?" Booker asked as he turned around to look at me. I hesitated, remembering some warnings we had been given about not discussing this work with each other, then motioned toward the door where the FBI agent sat reading a newspaper. I put my finger to my lips as a sign to be quiet. Booker saw my gaze and quietly stood and came back to my desk.

"What's up?" he asked me in a lowered voice.

Keeping my voice low, I said to him, "Look at this paste-up, Booker." I watched his face as he leaned over and studied the page in front of me. It was a diagram of military submarines and a section of the eastern coastline of the United States.

Booker raised his head and looked at me. I could see he was somewhat puzzled about what I was showing him.

"Do you know what this means, Booker?" I whispered.

He kept speaking low and answered. "Yeah, it looks like we've got subs protecting us right off our coast. Guess we can sleep well tonight." He turned to go back to his desk, and I grabbed his arm and stopped him.

"No, Booker, that's not what this diagram is. Read the caption that goes with it." I handed him the slip of photo paper I had typed that read, "*Seven Armed Russian Nuclear Submarines Stationed Off the Virginia Coastline.*" It was marked with a recent date.

"Holy shit!" Booker said loudly, and I shushed him again. "You've got to be kidding me!" He lowered his voice and looked closer at the diagram. "Goddamn, they're right at our door," he exclaimed.

"Shh, Booker," I said, touching his arm and pointing again at the guard outside the door. "We're not supposed to be discussing this, remember?" I quietly continued. "But no, I'm not kidding. That's not all. Take a look at this next diagram they just brought me." I pushed the paper toward him. It was a map of the eastern coastline with clusters of big black dots all over it. He stood there staring at it, trying to figure out what it showed.

Whispering low, I said, "Here, read the caption that goes with this diagram. It says, '*Destruction Area from Russian Nuclear Missile Strikes.*' This map shows the cities that would be destroyed, Booker. Do you see which one is right in the middle of the worst destruction?"

"Yeah," he answered, his eyes widening, "it's us, Washington, DC." He let out a long, ragged sigh. "Well, I'll be damned."

"No, Booker, it's, well, I would be toast! Now, how am I going to sleep tonight knowing all this? I have a family. Armed Russian subs are right off our coast, aiming their missiles our way, ready to fire them any minute. And can you imagine how much damage seven subs firing nuclear missiles at us would do?"

"Wow, I think I'll have a few drinks after work," Booker said. "Hell, I could use a few right now. Do you think those goons at the door would let us have a liquor delivery?" We looked at the guard by the door again, then made eye contact. We fell silent as the reality of what was actually going on in the United States at this moment sank in. We realized this was such grave, dangerous information to know. I bit my bottom lip, slowly shaking my head back and forth. Booker silently walked back to his desk with his shoulders slumped, lost in his thoughts.

When Dean came back into the room, we both stopped working and looked up at him. He paused, puzzled by our stare and silence, and asked, "Is everything okay?"

There was an uneasy quiet, then Booker said, "Yeah, we're okay. Josey and I are just thinking a vacation in Florida would be good to take right now."

Dean replied, "When we get this job done, we'll all have enough money to take a great vacation," and he sat down at his desk.

"Yeah, if there's a place left where we could go to," Booker said under his breath.

The Cold War tension between the United States and Russia had gone on for years, and there was no sign of it ending soon. It was no secret that we didn't like Russia, and the feeling was mutual. But having Russian subs positioned this close at this moment, able to fire missiles at us, was a vastly different and extremely dangerous thing. Our whole government and the seat of our military—the Pentagon—would be obliterated. It was difficult to keep working without thinking about those subs and the possibility of what they could do.

It reminded me of the Cuban Missile Crisis that President Kennedy had dealt with just a few years earlier, in 1962. The Russians had installed nuclear-armed missiles just ninety miles from the U.S. in Cuba. It was a tense time trying to get them removed. We thought we were on the brink of a nuclear war back then, but Kennedy handled it with a naval blockade and stern warnings that we would not tolerate missiles that close to our shore. He said we would use whatever military force we had to stop that threat. After a couple of weeks, Russia removed the missiles in exchange for us removing the blockade, our missiles from Turkey, and promising not to invade Cuba. The threat I was seeing now, just a few years later, seemed even more dangerous to me. They were even closer to our seat of government, and thousands of innocent people were in grave danger, including my family.

The next day, I resumed work on the top-secret publication, and more charts were delivered from technical. The new ones showed black symbols of our tactical jet fighters. They indicated the locations of the air force bases in the United States. Diagrams of aircraft carriers and submarine locations were delivered for paste-up too, and this time the photo caption I had typeset read, "*American Naval and Air Support.*"

As I put the pages together with their images, photo captions, and text, it became obvious that the publication was about an imminent Russian nuclear attack. Pages showed what the damage would be and what power we had to respond to their attack. It was shocking and unsettling news to me, and it would be shocking news to everyone else in the United States. Most Americans were consumed with the Vietnam War protests, the Civil Rights marches, the Women's Liberation Movement, plus the upcoming unusual presidential election. We were all still trying to recover from the tragic death of John Kennedy. All Americans were so preoccupied with all that activity happening around us. I felt sure no one had any clue the Russians were right off our shoreline, ready to wage war. Now I understood all the precautions the FBI was taking and the need for such tight security. I glanced over to where Lyla was working. She was concentrating on some papers and typing away. I felt the weight of guilt for what I knew about her lack of security clearance. I left work after that long day, troubled by what I had read and seen. I was also terrified for my family and my country.

That night in bed, my mind was so unsettled I just stared at the ceiling. Questions kept dominating my thoughts. *Will an attack from the Russians happen at any minute? The American people should know what's going on, so they can prepare. Shouldn't this be on the television news? Why isn't President Johnson telling the public? Kennedy told us when Russia had missiles right off the coast of Florida in Cuba. Should I tell Samuel about the secrets I read? Are we even safe in our apartment right now? I have to tell Samuel. No, I can't tell Samuel—I swore an oath to loyalty and secrecy not to talk to my spouse about anything I was working on. Is there someplace like a bomb shelter nearby where I can take the kids? Will I hear air raid sirens going off in time to get them there?*

Question after question pounded my brain like the brutal waves of a hurricane storm surge hitting the sand dunes on a beach and dragging them out into the darkness of the sea.

*If I tell anyone and the FBI finds out, we could all lose our jobs. Maria works so hard in the typesetting department while her husband fights in Vietnam, that wouldn't be fair to her. My bosses thought enough about my skills to give me this job. How can I betray that trust? But isn't it in the best interest of my fellow Americans to know what's going on? It might mean thousands of lives can be saved. Oh, God, what do I do?*

I thought about my coworkers who could have seen the diagrams. Then it dawned on me that I was the only one typesetting the headlines and photo captions. Right now, I might be the only one who would fully understand what the publication was about. The art department had made the drawings of the submarines, but they probably thought they were American subs. Technical had made charts of patterns, but when Cade delivered them to our room, he only said, "Here are some maps. I've no idea what they're for." Technical wouldn't understand the purpose of all the diagrams because they didn't have the descriptions that explained them. Maria and Lyla might be able to determine something from the text. However, they wouldn't have seen the diagrams to know where the subs were positioned or read the information in the captions. I had typeset all the captions and headings. Priscilla, our proofreader, would know everything when it was finished, because she would be reading the completed publication carefully. All my other coworkers were creating separate pieces and not seeing the complete pages. Dean, Booker, Priscilla, and I were the few people looking over the pages the president and his cabinet members would see. I fell into a fitful, uneasy sleep until Samuel came to bed.

The bedroom was dark and felt like a confessional, a place where I could voice all my secrets and fears. Samuel climbed into bed and settled down beside me. I started to speak, but he interrupted me by saying, "You'll never guess what happened at work today. I had a road call on a back road in Virginia. The truck ran out of power and shut right down, and the guy needed help fast. It was a refrigerated rig. I think he was carrying frozen chicken meat. Anyway, he wanted it fixed fast so his load wouldn't spoil. The driver had pulled off the road in a wide area by a field. At least I wasn't right out in traffic to work on it like on the Beltway. It was hotter than hell out there, though. I had to climb on top and under that engine. It took me some time to figure out the damn problem.

"I finally found a fuel line with a hole in it way underneath the cab. I was lying on the ground with my arms up in the engine, trying to connect a new section of the fuel line. My eyes saw something dark crawling on the frame by me. It was a damn snake! I jumped up so freakin' fast I hit my head trying to get out from under there. I stepped way back from the truck as the driver banged on the fender. The nasty snake dropped down and slithered away. He said it looked like a copperhead. They're quite poisonous. It probably wouldn't have killed me if I had gotten bitten, but it would hurt like hell. It can make you sick enough to throw up and have trouble breathing. God, I hate snakes! Those copperheads have a narrow neck area right behind their head so he could tell what it was. The damn thing might have bitten me any second. God, I'm so tired tonight. Really rough day today fighting traffic on the Beltway and almost getting bit by that shitty snake. I'm so glad to be home with you and the kids." He paused, let out a long sigh, then asked, "What was it you wanted to say?"

It was quiet for a few moments, then I softly answered, "Nothing right now, dear. Go to sleep." He leaned over and kissed me goodnight, and soon I heard his regular breathing. I lay there for a long time as Samuel slept. I was wide awake, trying to figure out how to keep us all safe and get out of the mess I was in.

## Chapter 9

I worked on that top-secret publication for days without talking to anyone about how conflicted I was. All that time, I weighed the pros and cons of what I should do about the information on those pages. I had sworn to secrecy, but knowing that millions of people were in such danger troubled me terribly. If a nuclear strike was imminent, they should prepare and find shelter. That included my own family. I loved them and worried about their safety more than anyone else. Yet, if I disclosed that information, I would lose my job. I could be prosecuted for breaking a sworn oath of secrecy to the government of the United States. My coworkers would surely lose their jobs if the FBI found out about Lyla. The agency would be sued, and any future government contracts would be canceled. I liked my job; I needed my job. I was still making monthly payments to the placement company for helping me find it. I finally decided that I must abide by that oath of secrecy. I wondered what other information was being kept from the American people. How many government contractors knew information that meant life or death for Americans and had to keep it silent?

Many believed our government was deceiving us about what was happening in Vietnam. The counts of soldiers killed over there were under suspicion for their accuracy. The fact that we were winning the war might be a lie too. I could not believe any news coming from our government. I changed my opinion of good ole honest Uncle Sam. He was dishonest, sneaky, and kept way too many secrets from us.

Newspapers were delving into the reasons why so many riots had broken out in the previous summer of 1967. It was believed that sweltering hot days and idleness had sparked some of them in Detroit, Newark, Minneapolis, and Milwaukee. Although rioting had stopped, police brutality in dealing with the rioters had enraged the protestors more. Police dogs, clubs, and powerful water cannons were being used on them. In the spring of 1968, Memphis garbage workers demonstrated for safer working conditions and higher pay. Sadly, two black sanitation workers were accidentally crushed to death in a defective compacter. They had taken refuge in it during a rainstorm. There was a history of other serious accidents happening there due to dangerous working conditions and faulty equipment. Television images of marches and protests going on in Memphis were broadcast almost every day. The sanitation workers received incredibly low pay. Their demands included a raise for the truck drivers and all the other sanitation workers. But they were refused any increase, which forced them to go on strike.

News stations showed mountains of garbage bags piling up on the sidewalks and rats tearing into them. People on the sidewalks had trouble walking around them. The sanitation workers were the subject of racial discrimination. Besides having unsafe working conditions, they were paid less than many white employees doing the same work. Their pleas for improvements and fairness with equal wages were ignored. After the workers formed their union, the mayor refused to negotiate with them. He refused to recognize their union and said the strike was illegal.

When Cade heard about the problems in Memphis, he commented, "If they didn't appreciate their sanitation job, maybe they could leave it and move up to gravedigger or toilet cleaner instead." He was such a disgusting racist and bigoted ass. I wondered how he became that way. Did he lay hold of that racism all on his own, or did it take hold of him? He made those comments right there in the layout department in front of Booker. I was angry at Cade, and at myself, too, because I was too timid to speak up and confront him about it. I was sure Cade did it to get a response from Booker, to get Booker fired. But Booker would just keep on working and never spoke up to Cade. Often, Booker left the room when Cade tossed out baiting insults like that.

Dean was checking pages we were working on and discovered that a diagram from technical was missing. He called Cade into our room and asked him where it was. Cade paused, then told Dean he had given the missing diagram to Booker earlier.

"I handed it right to him," Cade said.

"Is that true, Booker? Do you have it and accidentally left it out?" Dave asked him.

Booker looked straight at Cade's face, then back at Dave's, and said, "No, I never got that one. He never gave it to me."

Cade angrily said, "He's a liar! He's lost it and won't admit it! You ought to fire him. He doesn't belong here." Then he added, "He's incompetent."

The FBI man, hearing the commotion, leaned in and asked, "Is something wrong?"

Dean answered him quickly. "No, we're just handling some minor details. Everything is okay." Then firmly, he told Cade, "Find the goddamn diagram fast or make another even faster." Cade glared hatefully at Booker and left the room. Booker just got back to work on the page he was doing and shook his head back and forth without saying a word. My eyes met Dean's. I knew he felt the same as me at that moment. Cade had tried to get Booker fired once again.

When we moved down south, neither Samuel nor I knew that so much racial tensions had existed there. Our local newspapers had covered only some of the national news thoroughly. They covered the space program because we had manufacturing plants that did aerospace work, and IBM's home office was in the town where we lived. Those businesses thrived on big government contracts, and anything happening with IBM made it news of local interest that got printed on the front page of our papers.

So much of the local news was about the Vietnam War and protests happening all over our country. Many local men joined the service after being recruited at their high schools by different military branches. Recruiters came right into the schools to sign up young teenagers. For many, it was an opportunity to serve their country and start a career path.

We listened to Walter Cronkite faithfully every evening when he reported what was happening in Vietnam. We heard about the Flower Children in California and women protesting for equal pay and arguing over birth control rights. The television reporter covered the Cold War and what was going on in the space race with Russia. There was a lot of news to report during those times. So much upheaval was happening all over.

For some reason, though, the news of racial unrest, segregation, and double standards in many cities was not covered thoroughly by our local newspapers or newscasters. Perhaps it was because there was only a small black population in my hometown. We were walled off from all news of racial unrest by omission by local editors and broadcasters. It wasn't something our papers thought a local needed to know, I guess. News of racial problems down south was hidden in the back pages or not covered at all. We missed a lot of information about what was causing those widespread riots and protests. Now, living in Maryland, so close to DC, it seemed we didn't have to worry. All the chaos happening in Memphis and other cities was far away from us. We had believed we were safe where we were near our seat of government.

* * *

We worked until ten o'clock one night to finish the top-secret job and meet the crushing deadline for its printing. It was a dark, overcast night. I was warned not to go to the parking lot alone. Instead, I should have one of the guys escort me to my car.

"It's just not safe," Dean told me as he busily checked some pages we had just finished. "Don't do it, Country Girl. Don't go out alone anywhere here after dark. You're on Fourteenth Street now in the city." Wesley from technical was going to walk me to the parking lot, but instead, Booker asked if I could give him a ride since I would be traveling somewhat near his complex. He also said the buses were not running now, and no cab driver would pick up a young black man this late at night in DC. So, Booker was my security guard to walk me to the parking lot and would be my passenger. We didn't know each other well, so at first, it was a little awkward to be alone in the car so late at night. But we were coworkers and friends, and I sensed he was a good person. I had noticed that Booker always declined the offer when I asked him to go to lunch with us and wondered why. Maybe I could ask him about that on the way to his home.

Booker gave me directions to where he lived. From some news stories I had seen, I knew it wasn't a good section of DC. As I drove that way, I asked him, "Why do you live in the projects?"

"It's where I found a place with my family. It's not great, but we can afford it, and we're together."

"Can't you just leave and rent an apartment in a better area?"

"Country Girl, how many black people live in your complex?"

I thought about that question. It stunned me when I realized I had never seen a black family there or a black child at the pool. Astonished, I told him. "Now that you've made me think about it, I haven't seen any. Not a single one."

It hit me how little I knew about Booker, what he had experienced growing up, and what his life was like in DC. "Where are you from originally, Booker?" I asked.

"Miz-er-ee," he said, intentionally mispronouncing the state's name, "and I will never go back there again. At least I've got a good job at the agency. By the way, Country Girl, you don't have to ask me to go to lunch with you guys. They don't want me to. I'm what you call a 'token black' at that job so they can tell their clients they're equal opportunity employers and get the government jobs. That racist Cade is always causing trouble for me. I'd like to kick his ass one of these days, but it would get me fired."

"I've noticed he's always taunting and insulting you, and you show a lot of restraint. I can't stand the guy myself. I don't think the same way he does. I wasn't raised that way."

"I know that, Country Girl. Hell, you're giving me a ride to the projects, aren't you? How many others at the agency do you think would do that?" he asked. Secretly, I wondered if I was being dangerously naïve right now.

As we drove a few blocks closer to where Booker lived, we passed fenced and gated storefronts and buildings defaced with graffiti. Some stores had razor wire along the tops of their buildings. I didn't like the looks of the area we were entering.

"Booker, you could probably get a better job up north. There are companies like IBM and GE that would treat you fairly. You could get away from places like the projects."

"Country Girl, like I said, I've got family in there I take care of. I want to help them. That's why I be working so hard here and ignoring assholes like Cade," Booker replied.

Booker didn't realize it, but he had started talking differently away from the office. He was using plantation creole when he spoke now. I had learned about that form of speech in my high school English class. My teacher lived in the south for some time and was familiar with it. We were studying the present, past, and future tenses of verbs at that time.

"Down south, there's another tense in the English language," my teacher told us. "It's called the habitual tense. It isn't considered proper English, even though you hear it all the time down there. It's called plantation creole, a habitual tense. Some people say, '*I be going to the store*,' or if you ask what someone did last night, you'll hear '*I be watching Ed Sullivan*' and not the past tense, 'I was watching Ed Sullivan.' That's because colored people were always, always working."

Not *was working* or *will be working*, just *be* as in all the time—habitually. Thinking of what I had learned in that class made me realize again how different life was for Booker and others before him. It saddened me to realize how much had still not changed.

"Stop here," he said. "I live in that building over there." Booker pointed to an institutional-looking tall, red brick building several floors high. No Lady Bird landscaping surrounded those buildings to soften the hard edges. The place looked dismal. It did not look at all like what I would call a home.

"You live in there, Booker?" I asked him timidly. I couldn't imagine living in such a bleak-looking place. "I don't want to insult you, but that place looks scary."

"Yup, me and a whole lot of folks, along with the roaches and rats is livin' there," he answered.

"Why, Booker? You're an intelligent, hardworking man. Why can't you live in a friendlier and safer home than that? Why not try to get an apartment in a nicer neighborhood?"

"Country Girl, didn't you tell me one time you had lots of trouble finding a place to live when you moved down here? One you could afford and was where your family was comfortable?"

"Yeah, I did. It took us a while, but you could find one, too. They passed that Fair Housing Act, so you can't be discriminated against anymore," I told him.

"It ain't that easy. Those guys up on Capitol Hill can pass laws that say we can live on this block or that block, but it's the people who decide. They choose if the laws are going to be accepted and enforced, and lots of them are keeping their blocks for whites only. White blocks that black people are not welcomed to step one foot on. What we got when they freed us from the plantations was just a much bigger plantation, and now we have a lot more bosses." We both fell silent as I drove even closer to his address, then Booker said, "You can drop me off right here. I'll be getting out and walking the rest of the way."

"What? Don't be silly. I can take you closer to your door," I told him and kept moving my car forward.

"Country Girl, you don't want to go no closer. Listen to me. Boy, you are naïve, aren't you?"

"Booker, I don't understand. I can get you closer. It's late and dark. It's not a problem," I argued.

Booker reached over and gripped the steering wheel. "You stop right here, girl, and let me outta this car, then you turn 'round and go straight home," he said firmly. "If someone sees a white girl with a black man in here, we may both get dragged out of this car and hurt. I appreciate the lift, but you need to just stop here. I can walk. I'll be okay—this is my neighborhood."

At his insistence, I pulled over to the curb. Booker opened the door and got out, then said, "thank you," and he gently but firmly said, "you turn 'round now and don't go no closer. Thank you for the ride. I'll see you tomorrow." He watched me leave, then walked away toward the complex. I drove home, shaken and with a deeper impression of the dangers in DC than I had ever felt before.

I had been so clueless about how dreadful things were between the races in this divided city. It was being run by white government leaders. Earlier progress had been made when Thurgood Marshall was nominated as the first black judge to the Supreme Court. But so much more needed to be done to improve the lives of everyone. People of other races needed to be heard and included in the decisions our country made.

As I drove home, I thought about the news coverage for presidential candidate George Wallace, the governor of Alabama. I had quickly dismissed Wallace as a radical racist when I found out he so strongly supported segregation in schools and housing. In my opinion, there was no way he could get enough supporters to be elected. But, to my surprise, he had many people backing him. He was becoming a major threat to the Republican and Democratic candidates because of his many followers.

Wallace was an expert on how to play into people's fears during these turbulent times. He spoke out against the interference of big government in our lives, and many were listening to his message. He also took a hard stance against the demonstrators and rioters. Many people believed those protests were getting out of hand and wanted the police to be more forceful. They wanted the police to quell the disturbances quickly before they erupted into violence. Wallace became the voice of a white backlash against any civil disobedience or protests. He opposed their use of free speech and demonstrations in the streets and on campuses to get attention for their grievances.

Wallace constantly put himself forth as a patriot who loved America and was against federal intervention, including busing, to help obtain racial balance in schools. He told his supporters he would bring back law and order for Americans and that civil disobedience of any type would not be tolerated under his administration. All protestors should be locked up and prosecuted, he said. He pledged to make our schools safe and said he would clear Washington of liberals and end the Vietnam War.

One of the most effective tactics he used to win over supporters was an "us against them" theme. He said our enemies were anarchists, militants, college students, liberals, the press, and big government. He said they were all looking down their noses at the common man. He knew how to play the political game and glean supporters from the discontent and concerns of many.

I arrived home safely after dropping Booker off, and Samuel was waiting up for me. I told him about transporting Booker to the projects. He was concerned and told me never to do that again. "I heard some terrible things happen over there with drugs and violence. I don't want you going near that place again. Let one of the men give him a ride home next time," he said sternly.

I asked him how his day went to change the subject.

"Someone broke into the shop last night. He tried to rob the safe in the office," he told me.

"What? The shop where you work?"

"Yup, he's hamburger now."

"What do you mean he's hamburger?"

"They turn two guard dogs loose inside the building at night when the shop is closed. They're big, mean Dobermans, trained to attack. He must have tried to run from them because blood splatters were everywhere. The cops followed his trail to the bathroom where he was curled up like a baby, bloody as hell and sobbing."

"Was he hurt badly?"

"Yeah, he was all chewed up. I feel kind of sorry for him. He'll have those scars for life, but he got what he deserved, the stupid ass! He should have known better," Samuel said, shaking his head.

I couldn't help but remember how bad our finances were before we moved to Washington. We were on the verge of losing everything. Was this thief a common criminal, or did he desperately need money for his family? I had always been so quick to jump to judgment when I heard about a criminal. I believed that type had to be on drugs, enjoyed committing crimes, or was a sociopath. The man that broke into Samuel's shop did it at night when no one would be there. I remembered the gravedigger working at night, digging up bodies for jewelry at the wooded area our kids played in. The policeman had told us, "There are desperate people around here doing desperate things." Was that thief another desperate man needing money and had no means to earn it? Wow, I was in such a different environment than my hometown. I started thinking about Booker and how we are trained early to think and act in certain ways.

"Samuel, did you ever play a game when you were little where someone hid under a pile of leaves and then jumped out to catch you?"

"No, I didn't," he said.

"Well, I played a game like that with my brothers and sisters. In autumn, we'd work hard to get leaves raked up into a big pile that could completely cover one of us. Someone was chosen as 'It.' They were the person who hid under the pile of leaves we called the 'well.' A leader was a pretend mother. She told us supper was ready and to go wash our hands in the well. We would walk over and gather round the pile of leaves, pretending to clean our hands. Suddenly, the person hiding under those leaves would burst out and try to catch one of us. We would all run away screaming like bloody murder. Soon, the catcher, the person who was 'It,' would grab one of us and drag us back to the pile of leaves. That person would have to be the one hiding under the leaves next time. Do you know what that game was called?" I asked him.

"You know, I remember some of my classmates playing that game in elementary school on the playground," he answered, "although I can't remember the name of it."

"We called it 'Nigger-in-the-Well,'" I said sadly. "Now I wonder why it was called a name like that. Was it because of the Underground Railroad when negroes were hidden in places like wells? But if that was the reason, why was our catcher a scary bad person like a Boogie Man who would hurt us? How did that word get into my vocabulary when I was so young and only in elementary school? I lived in the north, far out in a rural area on a farm, a long way from the south. Did soldiers from World War Two bring that racism back with them for some reason and spread it? I guess I'll never know, but we were taught that game by other kids at our little country school. Strange, isn't it?" I asked. "And it was so unfair to the colored people and us."

"Josey, there are lots of things in this world that are so unfair. We were taught to play fair and be fair. 'Do unto others as you would have them do unto you.' Everyone learned that golden rule. But life isn't really like that, no matter how much we want it to be. Innocent children get horrible diseases or are born with lifelong health problems they suffer with. They don't deserve anything like that, and there's no way that's fair. Some people die before they even have a chance to fulfill their dreams or enjoy life. Some are born into crushing poverty and are abused for most of their lives. Life isn't fair; it can be terribly cruel and unfair. Many deserving people go without, and those that do not deserve anything because of the type of person they are or the choices they make seem to have everything. We should teach our children that instead of being fair—that life will be unfair to them. They must learn to cope with that when it happens because it will. Then they would be more prepared for what may come their way. Life just sucks sometimes."

"But Samuel, shouldn't we work to make life fairer for everyone? Wouldn't that make it a better world?"

"And how are you going to change natural events or stop poverty? How can you prevent people from being cruel to each other, Josey? It's an impossible job, and no one is God. There's no way we can stop those things for everyone. All we can do is try to help one person at a time when we can. Do something for someone else, even if it's in a small way. It might make a difference in their life. I still think it is much better to teach our children that bad things will happen to them and everyone. That's just the way life is and will always be. Bad things happen to good people through no fault of their own. Then they won't be so devastated when life isn't fair to them."

I fell asleep wishing for a better world for my children, all the other children, and for people like Booker and his family.

## Chapter 10

Walter Cronkite interrupted the program we were watching with a Special CBS News Bulletin. "Thursday evening, April 4, 1968, around six o'clock, a young father was standing on the second-floor balcony talking to friends by his motel room in Memphis, Tennessee. A shot from a rifle across the street struck him in the neck and killed him." It was Martin Luther King, Jr. He had been in Memphis a week earlier to participate in a march to support the sanitation workers who were striking. That march had erupted in some violence that King strongly opposed, Cronkite told us.

Dr. King always stressed peaceful nonviolence like Gandhi practiced, as a way to bring about change and social justice for colored people. He was upset that the previous march held in Memphis did not keep to those standards, so he returned a week later with the hope and intention of leading a second peaceful march.

"The shooter was an unknown white man who fled the scene," Walter Cronkite said. Dr. King was only thirty-nine years old and a husband and father. He was a beloved leader of his people and admired by others of all races. His courage, ideals, faith, and actions were examples to all of us. He worked to improve the lives of everyone during his brief time on this earth. Despite Dr. King warning others that he might be killed one day, his sudden, violent death shocked the nation.

I was terribly upset. I considered Dr. King to be a brave voice for human equality. He had withstood so much abuse. He had received many death threats but was still an example of protesting peacefully and having steadfast faith to evoke change. What was happening to our world, I wondered. Where were we headed as a country when our public leaders were killed so viciously? Just a few years earlier, John Kennedy, our president, had been assassinated in Texas. Controversial theories and questions still swirled around Kennedy's death that needed answers. For many people, the sorrow over that tragedy was still raw. A couple of years later, a black leader named Malcolm X was shot and killed by a Muslim assailant. He had been offended by what Malcolm X had said about different factions of the Muslim faith. Malcolm X was only thirty-nine years old.

Now, we were deeply involved in the Vietnam War with no quick end in sight. A war far from our country's shores. It was taking the lives of too many of our young men and women. The Vietnam War was so unpopular, especially among college-age students, that protest marches and sit-ins were constantly happening. Many young draftees were crossing the border for safety in Canada. President Johnson thought there should be a way to get more public support for the war. He didn't like all the bad press it was getting. He believed better press reports would perhaps stop some of the demonstrations against it. He called together a group of men nicknamed the "Wise Men." They were given the task of coming up with some ideas to make the war more popular. After that meeting by the Wise Men, war reports from Washington put a more positive spin on what was happening overseas. They kept reporting we were winning the war. The enemy was retreating, and our troops would be home soon.

None of that was true.

Walter Cronkite had spent time in Vietnam. One evening, he reported what he had seen. Just before his broadcast ended, he spoke honestly and directly to the American people. He said, "To say we are mired in a stalemate seems the only realistic, if unsatisfactory, conclusion." Then he added, "but it is increasingly clear to this reporter that the only rational way out then will be to negotiate, not as victors, but as an honorable people who lived up to their pledge to defend democracy and did the best they could." His words were sobering and contradicted the government's optimistic view of how we could and would win that war.

Not long after that broadcast aired, there was another shocking report. The number of body bags from the war in Vietnam was intentionally underreported, while the numbers of the enemy killed were highly exaggerated to the American people. As I listened to that broadcast, I wondered, "Body bags? What the hell is a body bag?" Then, a video clip came on of soldiers loading large black bags into the cargo hold of a huge airplane. It looked like they were stacking up piles of logs. But it deeply saddened me to find out they were the bodies of our soldiers who had lost their lives for us. Now, the shocking video evidence was there for everyone to see. The figures the government published were unreliable and false. We were certainly losing more of our young men and women than they were telling us.

Many protestors camped on the hard, stone steps of the Capitol building with signs, placards, and American flags. They tried to get the attention of the senators and representatives walking past them. Instead, they were ignored as if they were discarded litter from a lunchtime picnic. People just stepped around their bodies. Several protestors were wounded veterans on crutches with part of a leg missing or other serious injuries. Everyone wanted this war to be over. We had lost too many men and women and had gained so little. Now, someone had killed Martin Luther King, Jr., a good Christian man and recipient of the Nobel Peace Prize. The sadness of all the violence taking place in our world was overwhelming.

After we heard the news of Dr. King's death that Thursday night, we watched Robert Kennedy, President Kennedy's brother, bravely break the news to a black crowd in Indianapolis. "I have bad news for you, for all of our fellow citizens and people who love peace all over the world, and that is that Martin Luther King was shot and killed tonight." The crowd erupted into shrieks and moans. Kennedy continued to speak. "Martin Luther King dedicated his life to love and justice for his fellow human beings, and he died because of that effort. In this difficult day, in this difficult time for the United States, it is perhaps well to ask what kind of a nation we are and what direction we want to move in." Robert Kennedy was so sad; you could tell he was painfully thinking of his brother John. Robert knew the pain of a sudden, cruel, inhuman death.

President Lyndon Johnson spoke to the country the next day, asking them to reject the "blind violence" that had struck down Dr. King. DC Mayor Walter Washington appeared on television and called for calm and peace as Martin Luther King would have wanted. However, riots broke out in many cities. I became concerned when I found out there had been looting already in the district. Unlike Dr. King, Stokely Carmichael was a militant civil rights activist, and he and some others gathered at businesses in the Fourteenth and U, NW areas and urged them to close their doors in respect. The crowd with him started smashing windows at the People's Drug store. Carmichael supported rioting and incited their anger by telling them to go home and get their guns. Looting broke out and windows were smashed in many stores. Additional help for the police arrived, and by three o'clock in the morning, everything had calmed down. Samuel and I spent a troubled night worrying about what kind of world our two young children were growing up in.

The next morning, a Friday, we checked the local news report on the television to see what was happening. Everything was calm in the city, they reported. Some arrests had been made during the night, and now the police were positioned and ready to quickly stop any more trouble. The crowds had been dispersed, and there was no rioting or disturbances anywhere. Mayor Walter Washington ordered all the damage to be cleaned up right away. Everyone highly doubted there would be any more trouble. There were no warnings to stay inside, only to spend your day as usual. I left for work, glad, like others, that the rioting was over and done with. I was ready to finish the week and then relax over the weekend.

It was a quiet, normal drive to the agency. DC was a city where no one thought serious trouble could ever happen. There was a strong military presence at Fort Belvoir nearby. The city also had local DC police and federal Park Police. On top of that, the president lived here with his protective security personnel. Plus, there was the Pentagon based nearby with all its military personnel. If any city had numerous protective security forces, it was DC.

I was working at my desk early Friday, sipping my morning cup of coffee and doing my work as usual. In Washington that morning, Stokely Carmichael had a rally at ten o'clock and spoke to a large crowd. He told them, "White America has declared war on black America," and called them to action. Shortly after that, the rioting began again. Booker was out of the room, and Cade came crashing in and announced to us all, "I just heard on the radio that the sons of bitches are lying down in the road, blocking traffic!"

"What, Cade? Who's lying down in the road where?" Dean asked, concerned.

"The n_____s" he said, "laying right down on the road so cars can't go by them, further up from us on Fourteenth and U," he said, pointing north of us. "They're blocking traffic. Let them lay down in front of me—I'll gladly run right over the sons of bitches," he answered with a sneer. He took a big puff of his cigarette and blew the smoke out, sticking his nose in the air as he did. Dean shook his head as he turned away from Cade.

*God, I cannot stand him,* I thought. *He's such a racist pig. How much of what he says can we ever believe? He has never been a purveyor of truth. Why should we listen to him now?*

Dean said, "I'll turn on my radio so we can find out what's happening." He looked toward the window. "If the looting starts again, it could get bad for us here."

He cranked up the volume on his Emerson radio. We stopped work and gathered around it, silently listening to the latest news updates breaking into the music. The reporter said that widespread looting was happening right now. Rioters were breaking windows of stores and carrying off everything they could. The liquor stores were being hit the hardest. The police were on the scene, using tear gas and trying to contain the mobs in the streets, but they were being overwhelmed. We looked at each other as we listened, speechless except for Cade. Of course, he kept making his ugly comments. "Goddamn troublemakers. Who the hell do they think they are?"

"Don't we have a television here somewhere?" I asked. "I'd like to see what Walter Cronkite is reporting. He usually gives us the truth."

Dean answered, "The only one with a television in his office is Mr. Stevens, and I don't think he would be happy if we asked to watch television instead of working."

"The area where they're looting is several blocks from here," Dean said. "I think we'll be fine. It sounds like the problems are all up there. We should be safe where we are." Then he added, "I feel sorry for them. They have a right to be angry and devastated at the killing of Dr. King. I'm angry too."

"He was the biggest troublemaker of all!" Cade said forcefully. "They can be as angry as hell if they want to. That doesn't mean they can destroy property and steal anything they get their thieving hands on." He was silent for a moment and added, "Wait, a minute . . . hell, let them destroy their stores, burn them all down if they want. Burn their apartments, too. They won't be living here after that, will they?" He seemed almost happy now with the prospect of fires and destruction in those blocks of DC.

"Don't you have work to do in technical?" Dean asked Cade angrily. "And Cade? It's negroes or black people, you got that? I don't want to hear you talking like that again," he told him forcefully as Cade turned his back and left the room.

We returned to work at our desks, and silence fell over us as we listened to the latest breaking news reports on the radio, accompanied by the sound of sirens going past our block. By lunchtime, there was a report of several buildings completely engulfed with fire. The firefighters were being attacked with rocks and bottles thrown at them. They had to pull back and could not respond to keep the fires from spreading to other buildings. We looked up the street from our second-floor windows and saw huge plumes of black smoke billowing up into the sky five or six blocks away. It was just after lunch and the riots were in full force by then. It became apparent to us that we were not as safe as we thought. Reports came over the radio that snipers were shooting at police and firefighters from some rooftops. All help to quench the fires and rioting had to retreat. The protests and the destruction were now out of control.

By then, we all wanted to leave the building and go home. The wind blew the smell of smoke our way, and the sound of sirens was almost constant. Fire trucks, ambulances, and police cars raced up and down the streets. The radio announcer said everyone would be safer indoors, to stay off the streets. A report of white people being dragged from their cars and beaten came over the radio. I was terrified. I wanted to get out of there and be safe in my apartment with Samuel, far away from the city.

Word came that our boss was talking to the police on the phone and getting information on what we should do. He came upstairs with our receptionist. She jotted down notes on a steno pad as she followed tight on his heels. With a worried look, he told us the police said the National Guard had been called out, and troops were coming from Fort Belvoir to help evacuate people. They told him we must all stay where we were. Do not try to leave the building by ourselves or even in a group. Help was on the way. We were to return to work for now. He turned around and left, and we overheard him giving orders to our receptionist to get all the accounts due records together. We took turns using the few phones in the different departments to call our spouses or family. But the lines were jammed, and no calls could go out or come in.

The radio reporter said, "The fires and rioting are out of control now and spreading to other blocks as the size of the mob continues to grow." At times we heard sporadic gunfire but didn't know if it was tear gas or real ammunition or who was using it. We didn't want to stay at the agency, but we couldn't go outside either. We were trapped. No one could focus on work now. We only paced around, got more coffee, and worried about what to do. An eerie quiet settled over us as we thought about the fires and possibly being trapped in our building. Cade lamented how "he wished he had brought his guns to work that day." I packed everything in my desk drawer and on my drafting table and put it into my briefcase just to keep busy. Or maybe I had a premonition.

My greatest fear was that we could not get out of the building before dark. *What will happen to us then? Will the mobs come down the street where we are? There's nothing of interest to looters here, but they have so much anger against whites right now. Who knows what they might do? Will our building catch on fire? Will the mob drag us outside and beat or kill us in their rage?*

As the hours passed, my fears grew stronger. We felt a little relief when our boss told us that army troops had blockaded the intersection above our street. Armed soldiers were there with machine guns in case the mob came any closer.

He added that the military had set up an escape route for us. "Go to your cars together as a group and line up in a convoy," he told us. My dream job at the agency had turned into a hellish nightmare. I hugged Maria and Lyla, and we said goodbye.

"Hurry!" our bosses told us, and no one had a problem with that. We were packed and ready to leave as soon as the opportunity came. Everyone said, "Be careful, be safe, and see you next Monday when all this craziness is over." A soldier with a rifle over his shoulder held the door to our building open as we hurriedly exited and went to our cars. As I started my car, I noticed my hand trembling as I tried to put the key in the ignition. When I pressed the gas pedal, my knee shook so much that I had to grip my kneecap to steady it. I kept repeating, *calm down, calm down, help is here, you're going home.*

I eased my car out of the lot and pulled into line with the others. I saw soldiers everywhere holding rifles with bayonets fixed on the ends. There were jeeps full of soldiers blockading several intersections nearby and the eerie sight of a tank in the street. I could see more frightened employees streaming out of other buildings on our block with the help of the military and going to their cars. It was shocking to see how different it looked from only a few hours earlier when I had come to work. After everyone was lined up, the soldiers led us south on Fourteenth Street, away from the fires and chaos. We traveled through red lights as if we were in a funeral procession. The military riding in the jeeps that led us had rifles pointing in all directions. The convoy moved fast, and it didn't take long to get several blocks south before the lead jeep pulled over and motioned us to keep going.

This was my normal route from work to home, and soon I headed back through familiar neighborhoods toward our apartment. As I crossed over into Maryland and neared Bladensburg, it became surreal how different it was. People casually walked their dogs, kids played outside, and the sun shone in a smoke-free sky.

I wanted to scream, "Don't you know what is going on back there?!" But all I could do was weep and try to concentrate on driving as tears flowed freely down my face. I wanted to be with my husband. I wanted to hug my children and know they were safe. I wanted to be inside my apartment and lock that stupid heavy metal door. There was a war going on back there, but only blocks away, people were stopping at gas stations as usual, and chatting, and no one seemed concerned. Everything in the suburbs appeared perfectly normal. *But are my children and my husband okay?* I wondered.

By the time I parked my car and went into our apartment, I was a mess. Samuel had heard about the trouble down on Fourteenth Street and was worried about me. I broke down as soon as I saw him, and he held me tight.

"I couldn't call you," I said. "The phone lines were jammed."

"I know, I know. I tried to get through to you several times, but no luck. Thank God you're home now and safe," he told me. I told him everything that had happened and filled him in on what it looked like back at work.

"God, I didn't know it was that bad. I've been watching some reports on television, but they didn't show all that. I had no idea of all the military presence. You even saw a tank in the street?"

"Yes, I did. And soldiers with guns and bayonets. Sandbags were piled up at street intersections like a kid's fort, only with soldiers manning them with real machine guns. It was like being in a war. So many buildings are burning! Dark, billowing black smoke is everywhere. We kept hearing gunshots, and they kept getting closer to us. What am I going to do if the mobs burn the agency down? You know I need that job. People are getting hurt back there. It's so terrible. There's so much fire and smoke, and gunshots, and sirens!" I said, still shaking.

"It will be okay," Samuel said. "You'll probably be back at work Monday morning. There have been riots before. Someone said they always shut them down before it gets too widespread. Then everything goes back to normal, just wait and see."

I silently thought about what I had seen and been through that day and felt it was different this time. Then I told him, "I'm not sure I want to go back there, Samuel. I'm glad it's Friday, and I won't have to make that decision until Monday morning."

Later, after we put the children to bed, we sat together watching the news. The rioting hadn't stopped. It had spread out into an even wider area. Many more buildings were burning, and more troops were called in to try and contain the rioters. Mayor Walter Washington announced a strict curfew. Anyone violating it would be arrested and jailed.

Hundreds were injured before it was over, and several died in the chaos. The Marines set up stations on the steps of the Capitol with mounted machine guns, and army troops ringed the White House, guarding it. The chaos continued Saturday and Sunday until finally, the fury of the rioters were satiated, and it stopped. The toll was thirteen dead by fires or by being shot by police or rioters, 1,097 people had been injured, and over 1,000 businesses and buildings were destroyed. It took almost 12,000 federal troops and 1,750 National Guard to control the mobs. Rioting got within two blocks of the White House before the angry mob was forced to retreat.

Sunday evening, after the children went to bed, Samuel and I talked late into the night. I had made a phone call and found out our block had not been damaged or torched, but I couldn't bring myself to go back there even if it was untouched. I could never feel safe working there again or going out to lunch with my coworkers. I called in early Monday morning and told Ted I would not return.

"Are you sure?" he asked. "I'm sorry to hear that. You're such a good worker. We would like to keep you. Don't you want to think about it for a few more days?"

I answered him, "Yes, I'm sure, Mr. Wickham. I'm so sorry. I loved my job, and you have been a good boss, but I don't feel safe returning there."

"I do understand," he said. "There are a couple of others who aren't coming back. I'll give you a good reference."

"Thank you for that," I told him. "And thank you for taking a chance on hiring me. I appreciate what you did and have learned a lot."

"Well, give us a call if you change your mind. We'd like to have you come back," he finished saying before we both hung up.

My decision made me sad, but I felt a deep sense of relief, too. I would not have to go anywhere near the riot area again. Samuel was covering for someone else that Monday and had to work the early shift. He kissed me goodbye and told me to cheer up. He was sure things would get better now that the rioters had finished venting their anger. "Relax, okay? You've been through a lot. It'll be better now—you'll see. Enjoy your day, hon, okay?" he said, smiling at me as he left.

"I'll try to," I told him.

Minutes later, he came back through the door, outraged, talking loudly. "I don't believe this shit!"

"What's wrong? Why haven't you left for work?"

"Every goddamn windshield on every goddamn car in that lot has been smashed with rocks."

"No! You're kidding me! Our car too?"

"Damn right, our car too. Now, what are we going to do? The glass is so smashed I have to get that windshield replaced before I can drive anywhere. I'll have to call the insurance company. Do you know if we have a deductible on glass replacement? I'm gonna call the police to report it. I don't think too many others know about their windshields yet. They're probably just getting up. What a hell of a way to start a Monday!" he said, disgusted, as he dug into his wallet for the insurance card and reached for the phone.

It bothered me that someone that angry, or perhaps even a group of enraged people, had been so close to us while we slept. Why did they feel they must smash all the car windshields? Who did that, and where were they now? The police came and wrote down details of the damage. Big rocks were still lying on some caved-in windshields and hoods, so they knew they were used. Finding the culprits was another thing. Remarkably, no one had seen or heard anything happening during the night. Auto glass repair trucks soon arrived. Workmen were busy removing the broken glass and replacing it with new windshields. The owners stood around in huddled groups, talking angrily about the damage to their cars. As soon as the new windshields were in, those waiting jumped in their vehicles and took off for work. When our car was ready, Samuel kissed me goodbye again and said, "Be sure and lock the door behind me. All those locks, Josey. Call me right away if you have any problems. I'll only be a few blocks away."

When he left, I locked the metal door and let out a big sigh as I leaned against it. Now I had to get in touch with the office at Bladensburg Elementary School. They assured me it was safe to have the children come to class. The buses were running, and there were absolutely no problems. It seemed like all the mothers stood in the parking lot when the bus pulled in that morning to see our children off to school. Everyone came back to collect their children later in the afternoon when it returned. No longer did only a couple of parents acting as parking lot chaperones greet them and escort them to their apartments. Every single child had a family member there to meet them and take them to their home. We were all so concerned about our children's safety after what had happened in DC.

Later in the week, the television news covered Martin Luther King, Jr.'s funeral procession. It traveled from a family service at the Baptist church in Atlanta, where he had been a pastor, to Morehouse College for the public funeral. The three-mile procession was lined with hundreds of thousands of distraught mourners and thousands more watched on television. His casket rested on a simple wooden farm wagon drawn by a couple of mules. Lester Maddox, the governor of Georgia, refused to lower the state flags to half-staff, but a directive from the federal government forced him to do so. Despite Martin Luther King, Jr. being loved and admired by thousands, Maddox also refused to allow King's body to lay in state in Georgia. He said he was "an enemy of the country."

Martin Luther King, Jr. had numerous death threats against him during his lifetime. Before his death, when talking about his funeral, he said he did not want his awards and honors to be mentioned. Instead, he wanted it to be said that he tried to feed the hungry, love and serve humanity, and clothe the naked. At the end of the services, a large crowd sang "We Shall Overcome."

Robert Kennedy and his wife, Ethel, attended the services. I could not help but remember how different his brother's funeral had been, just a few short years earlier. John Kennedy's body had been moved in a horse-drawn caisson, and over 300,000 people watched as it traveled to the Capitol Rotunda to lay in state. During the cortege, the crowd remained silent. All you heard was the muffled drums and the sound of the horses' hooves on the pavement as we mourned his passing. A spirited black horse was saddled for the procession, but symbolically, its rider was gone. When the casket was moved from the cathedral after the service, Jackie, Caroline, and John Jr. stood at the top of the steps. The sad image of three-year-old John Jr., who raised his little hand and saluted his father's coffin, will remain in my mind forever. It was even sadder because it was his birthday. We had said goodbye to the shocking early deaths of men we admired. They had been working to make life better for us and others. Everyone seemed to be holding their breath. We all wondered what could possibly happen next.

# Chapter 11

Before another week passed in April, I started a job in Bel Air, Maryland. It was closer to our apartment than my DC job, with an easier commute than traveling into the city. I no longer needed to negotiate my way through those embassy areas where the diplomatic limousines constantly double parked. It wasn't a prestigious job like working in an advertising agency. Now, I worked in a technical drafting department doing inking on drafting satin with Radiograph pens for charts, graphs, and diagrams using triangles, French curves, and all sorts of templates. It was the kind of work Cade had done at the agency. I was disappointed that it wasn't a paste-up position. There was no possibility of any creative work with my new employer, but I had a job with good pay and benefits. Also, it was far from Fourteenth Street and in a safer area, and Cade did not work there. That was a big plus.

Samuel took us out to a well-known seafood restaurant to celebrate. It was famous for its Maryland crab cakes and other fresh seafood. We were reading the menu and trying to decide what to order. I encouraged Samuel to try something different from what he usually ate. "Why don't you get the Blue Crab meal, Samuel?" I asked him. "It's a popular meal in Maryland. They give you a platter of them to eat. Be courageous—try eating something you never tasted before. I like Chinese food now that I tried it with my friends from the agency."

"Hmm, I don't know about ordering crab like that. I think they give you a hammer or something, and you have to crack them open yourself. You know I don't like food like shrimp that comes with its own crispy, inedible wrapper. I hate doing that fussy stuff of peeling those shells away to get at the little morsels of meat. Give me a big juicy grilled steak I can sink my teeth into and a beer and I'm a happy man," he said, smiling.

"You're a hopeless redneck, Samuel," I told him, laughing, "but I love you anyway. I think I'm going to try the Blue Crab platter. I've heard it's very good when you dip the meat in the melted butter they serve it with. Why don't you at least try the crab cakes they're famous for? I think you'll like them."

Samuel did order a crab cake sandwich on a toasted roll with a stuffed baked potato and coleslaw, and he enjoyed it. Our children had breaded shrimp with French fries they dipped in ketchup. They liked that the shrimp came with tail handles and they could eat everything with their fingers.

I thought the Blue Crab was delicious even though I had to use a bunch of tools like a surgeon to get at the meat. First, the waitress encouraged me to put a bib on because it would be messy. She gave me a mallet, a knife, and a sharp metal pick and showed me how to attack the crab shell with those tools and use the pick to get out the meat. It tasted delicious, and all the work was well worth it. The children laughed at Mommy wearing a bib and getting her hands all messy. I had melted butter dripping off my chin before I was done. During that dinner, having fun with Samuel and the children, I forgot all about the recent events that had been so upsetting.

Washington, DC, simmered down after the rioters vented their rage, as predicted. But there remained a silent undercurrent of tension that was constantly there. The extra troops that had been called out left, the federal Park Police returned to their usual posts helping confused or lost tourists with directions, and the government resumed daily operations at the Capitol and White House. War protestors returned to the steps of the Capitol for the senators and representatives to walk around and continue to ignore. The reality of the loss of life, injuries, and damage to apartments, workplaces, and shopping areas was sobering to the black community. Blocks and blocks of buildings stood as blackened, broken skeletons or smoldering piles of debris. So many buildings had been burned or destroyed by the 20,000 rioters. People started trying to rebuild their lives soon after and get back to whatever was "normal." I settled into my new job in Bel Air the best I could. It was work and I would have a weekly paycheck. It was not interesting art to do, but I needed to keep working for my children and Samuel. He had a good job with a future at Mack Trucks and wanted to stay there. April passed, and then May, and soon Grace would graduate from kindergarten, which was a huge milestone for our little family.

Then another protest incident happened in DC. Everyone warned us to stay away from the National Mall. A tent city had been hastily erected down there with hundreds of activists living in it. On the south side of the land that flanked the reflecting pool, over 3,000 people were living in A-frame-style tents constructed from plywood, plastic sheeting, and canvas.

They named it Resurrection City, and it was part of the Poor People's Campaign. It had been Martin Luther King's idea to bring attention to the hunger, malnutrition, and poverty so many suffered in our country. The plan to build the tent city in Washington, DC, had been put on hold after his death. But members of the Southern Christian Leaders' Conference decided to go forth with it a few weeks later. They wanted to make people aware of the inequality in income and the racism against black people and others in the United States. The camp had been populated with other impoverished races who had similar problems. There were Hispanics, Native Americans, Puerto Ricans, and even white coal miners from Kentucky and Hispanic farmworkers from California. The camp boasted of a city hall, a mess tent, general store, health clinic, and even a free barbershop for the people living there.

Its purpose was to provide a place for poor people and activists to live and go out daily to picket and meet with elected officials in the Senate and House of Representatives, as well as the heads of various government departments, to present their demands and grievances. The Southern Christian Leadership Conference was granted a permit to camp on the National Mall. However, there were limits on how many could stay there, and the time allotted to camp was only six weeks. The protestors wanted laws passed that provided a living wage for underprivileged working people of all ethnicities, job training, and financial protection for small farmers. They wanted food stamps available and school lunch programs for poor children who had nothing to eat. They believed our affluent nation, with its advanced medical capabilities, should be more accessible to the poor. They also wanted to inoculate our vulnerable children against diseases. And they wanted to know why teaching materials and proper education were not available to all American children equally. Another concern was why no real progress had taken place in desegregating schools, workplaces, and housing.

Local residents, like Samuel and me, were still on edge after the recent riots and the killing of Dr. King. People feared the camp would keep getting larger and that rioting would break out again in the district. However, this time it would be much closer to the White House. Samuel and I heard reports of arguments and thefts that had taken place in the camp. Some people staying there had been arrested. We kept far away from that area and only watched the happenings on television. President Johnson activated 20,000 soldiers just in case the protestors decided to take over the nation's capital. Rumors spread that black militants had infiltrated the peaceful protestors' camp, and more trouble was likely to happen. "Black Power" was painted on some structures in the camp. That phrase alarmed many as to what it could possibly mean. Tensions rose to the surface again in the district.

On June 5, American citizens, including those living in Resurrection City, were stunned by the news that one of our leaders had suffered another tragic death. Robert Kennedy, brother of President John Kennedy, had been shot and killed. He had recently won the Democratic primary in the state of California. He might have become our next president because he was so popular. President Lyndon Johnson had been unsuccessful in ending the war in Vietnam, so back in March 1968, he announced he wouldn't run for president again. When he took office in 1963, he announced "A War on Poverty." Nothing had been accomplished with that effort, though. That war on poverty had been put on the back burner to deal with the Vietnam War instead.

Candidate Bobby Kennedy was loved by many, and his campaign for president was well supported, not only because he was John Kennedy's brother and had shown great composure and courage during the time of John's assassination, but also because they felt he would unify our divided country. Minorities admired him for his steadfast loyalty to helping the cause of civil rights for everyone and his campaign to help the poor.

Robert was exiting the Ambassador Hotel when a twenty-two-year-old Palestinian named Sirhan Sirhan shot him. The doctors worked for four hours trying to save his life, but he died the next day. It was another shocking, heartbreaking loss for our country when our hearts were so raw with all the other recent losses. He was only forty-two years old, a husband to Ethel, and a father of ten children. Ethel was three months pregnant with their eleventh child at the time of his death. During his lifetime, Robert had fought against organized crime. He went to South Africa in 1966 to speak against Apartheid. He spoke there about hope for change in the world and said, "Each time a man stands up for an ideal, or acts to improve the lot of others, or strikes out against injustice, he sends forth a tiny ripple of hope, and crossing each other from a million different centers of energy and daring, those ripples build a current that can sweep down the mightiest walls of oppression and resistance."

Bobby Kennedy also visited the poorest Americans and saw poverty at its worse and children with swollen bellies and open sores. He said, "It's terrible to have all this in a country as affluent as ours." He traveled to see the poor in the Mississippi Delta and the families in the produce fields of California. He talked firsthand with those living on Indian reservations and those in remote coal mining communities of Appalachia. With sincerity, he told the press, "I love these people." He gave us all hope for a brighter future when everything seemed so hopeless.

His death was another devastating blow to our morale. I felt like our world, the world I had grown up in, would never be the same. Our leaders were being killed in our own country in the prime of their lives. It was almost as if we lived in some third-world country run by dictators instead of the United States of America. We were in an unpopular war in Vietnam that we could not win. Our young people were losing their lives or becoming crippled mentally and physically in that war, and the government was purposely altering the numbers of true data about what was happening over there and lying to us. Even the dreams of an exciting space program to explore the galaxy and land a man on the moon were in jeopardy. Racism, segregated neighborhoods, and schools still existed, with no hope that it would soon change for the better. And there remained so much violence and anger across the nation, for one reason or another. A foreboding of hopelessness hovered over us all at these troubled times. It was difficult to imagine things would get better and believe in the American Dream. It was easier to just accept that we now lived in a dangerous, unfair world. That golden rule of "Do unto others as you would have them do unto you" seemed to no longer be in practice. We were left with the day-to-day sense that life is unfair and another terrible thing was sure to happen at any moment.

I was just hanging in there emotionally after what happened to my friend Hope. The terror of going through the riots added greatly to my sadness and stress. I had hoped that time would help me put it all behind me. I no longer worked near the blocks that were destroyed by the riots in DC, but I remained uncomfortable shopping for groceries or doing any usual activities I had done so carelessly and easily before. Since Hope and Eli had left, Samuel and I had not even gone on our usual weekend outings with the kids to see the sights. I missed Maria, Dean, Booker, and even Lyla at the agency and the carefree fun we experienced going out to lunch together and laughing. The joy of living in an exciting new place and working my dream job had been swept away. The torrent of riots and assassinations had replaced it with a strong hesitation to go anywhere that was crowded. Now, I never wanted to go out after dark for any reason.

I had a shorter drive to work, but the streets were still jammed with commuters every morning rushing to make it to their jobs on time. I was running late one day and going as fast as traffic allowed when I noticed the red light on the dash, signaling that I needed to get gas. "Not now!" I said, annoyed. "Give me a break, will ya? I haven't got time for this!" I yelled at the car as if it could understand my frustration and do something.

I knew I must stop because I wasn't sure how long that darn light had been on. I seldom paid attention to the dials or lights on the dash. I relied on Samuel to monitor the car's needs. I watched for a gas station as I pulled forward with all the other traffic as if we were linked in a fast-moving, invisible chain. I finally spotted a station coming up on my right side, broke my link to the others, then pulled in beside a pump.

An attendant came out and asked, "How much you want, lady?" Then he started pumping the gas and came back around to wash my windshield while my car was filling.

He finished pumping the gas and asked if I wanted him to check the oil in my engine, to which I replied, "No, thanks, I'm in a hurry." I paid him, pulled my car away from the pump, and waited at the edge of the driveway for a break in the line of speeding commuter traffic. There were bumper-to-bumper cars, as far as I could see, with no openings to get back out. I eased the car as far forward as possible so I would be ready when that opening came. *I'll probably have to floor it,* I thought. Everyone sped by so fast that I worried about not getting back in line.

As I waited, I saw a movement off to my left on my side of the sidewalk further down the street. It was a man with what looked like a big plastic garbage bag flung over his shoulder, walking toward me. My car blocked the sidewalk as I waited for that opening in traffic.

"Come on, people, let me out," I said out loud as I pounded my fingers on the steering wheel. "I have to get to work too." My window was partially down, but there was no way those drivers could hear me. The man with the garbage bag was coming closer and would be near my car soon. He would have to walk around the back of my car, I thought, and I kept watching traffic. I glanced in my rearview mirror. Darn, another car was tight on my bumper, waiting to leave the station too. The man had almost reached my car door now. I could see he was a young man with what now looked like a full bag of laundry over his shoulder. He was not happy I was blocking the sidewalk. He came close, stopped right beside my door, and glared angrily at me. Then he said, "Move it, bitch!"

Frightened, I answered, "I'm trying to move. I'm trying. There aren't any openings in this traffic!"

With that answer, he stepped even closer, pulled a knife out of his pocket, pointed it at me, and said, "Move it now, bitch, or I'm going to cut you!"

Terrified, I immediately locked my door and rolled up my window. Then, seeing a ridiculously small opening between the oncoming cars, I floored the gas pedal and prayed I would squeeze in between them. I braced myself for the crunch of metal. Tires screeched and horns blared, but incredibly I had made it. I was shaken. I had looked into the eyes of hatred toward me that chilled my soul to its core. There was no doubt in my mind that he would have hurt me.

It was hard to focus on work that day. The frightening incident with the young man haunted me. I had never seen such hatred and anger in the eyes of anyone like that before. I told Samuel about it when I returned home, and he was quite upset about it too. We both thought I would be safe with my new job away from downtown DC, but I wasn't. He wanted me to quit working. I couldn't do that with our obligations. I just needed to steel myself against my fears and be careful and vigilant about my surroundings at all times.

I read up on safety tips for women and how to defend myself against an attacker. One of the tips it mentioned was to stomp on their foot if they grab you from behind. Another was to have your keys out and ready to open your car or house door, so you can use that key to jab attackers in the eye if needed. It warned to be aware of my surroundings and others around me. It was difficult for me to be so distrustful of everyone. I just wanted to do the opposite as I had always done. I wanted to be trusting and leave my door unlocked and go out after dark, but I was too naïve in the city. I made sure I would not run out of gas again. It wasn't just angry black men I needed to fear. A white man had attacked Hope. Samuel and I continued our schedules of working different shifts, and a couple of weeks passed without any more incidents.

Resurrection City on the National Mall had used up its permit for the camping and got a few more days' extension, but even that extra time had run out. Staying there was miserable for the protestors. It rained for twenty out of the forty-one days since they put the tents up. At times, the rain was torrential, and the camp was mired in mud and standing water, causing terrible living conditions. Several of the Hispanic activists chose to stay at the Hawthorne School instead. They were the only ones sheltered from the mud and rain.

On June 19, fifty to one hundred thousand people participated in the Solidarity Day March in DC. Speakers stood on the steps of the Lincoln Memorial, in front of the seated statue of Lincoln, and addressed the crowds. They included Coretta Scott King, Reverend Abernathy, Eugene McCarthy, and Hubert Humphrey. Even the United Auto Workers Union was represented and showed support for the people of Resurrection City and the changes they were trying to accomplish for the poorest Americans.

There had always been a large police presence around the camp since its beginning, and on June 20, some members of the NAACP from Milwaukee threw rocks at them. The police responded by firing tear gas into the cluster of plywood buildings, and they ordered everyone to leave immediately.

Many were still staying in the hastily erected shelters, and it was no longer a safe place to be. A white visitor was beaten, shot, and robbed on June 23. In another incident, it was believed some youths from Resurrection City had thrown firebombs at cars going by the camping site. Tear gas was fired into the encampment again, and heavy clouds caused men, women, and children to choke and gag on the noxious fumes, so many left. Soon after that, knowing that the remaining protestors must leave or be arrested, Reverend Abernathy gathered those who wanted to leave peacefully, and they marched to a place where they could voluntarily turn themselves in. Still, some remained in Resurrection City and refused to move out. Over a thousand officers, called the Civil Disturbance Squad, took on the job of clearing the remaining stubborn protestors out of the camp. They searched all the Resurrection City shelters and made more arrests. Not long after that, government workers tore down all the shelters. They hauled away plywood, canvas, plastic sheets, personal items, protest signs, and anything the protestors left behind. It was extremely difficult for those that camped there, were arrested, and released. Many never lived or traveled in Washington, DC, and didn't know their way around the city. They were poor and destitute, with no place to go now that their shelters were gone. They had no means to get back to their hometowns across the United States. Most had been bused into Washington for free, but there was no help when it came time to go back home.

Just a few days after all that chaos of clearing out the camp at the National Mall, I was lying in bed late at night. The alarm clock loudly ticked off minutes on the table beside me. Our children were in bed, and Samuel lay sound asleep beside me, but I couldn't close my eyes. My mind was deeply troubled.

Pictures flashed through my head as if I sat in front of a television, flipping through channels. Scenes of John Kennedy and his brother Robert's deaths came into view, one after another. I thought about the Civil Rights marchers and seeing rocks and bricks thrown at them. I remembered images of powerful water cannons violently knocking people down and police swinging clubs at protestors and vicious dogs attacking unarmed people. I saw shadowy pictures of Martin Luther King's funeral in my head and remembered our visit to the Lincoln Memorial and reading Lincoln's engraved words: "And dedicated to the proposition that all men are created equal." Lincoln had spoken those words, hoping that every race of people would be treated with honor and dignity and have opportunities and respect instead of usury and abuse.

Pictures of women marching with signs that said, "Equal Pay for Equal Work" and "Women Have Rights Too," flashed on my mental screen. Wounded soldiers holding American flags and peace signs sitting on the steps of the Capitol as senators and representatives passed by, acting as if the veterans did not exist, came into view. I knew I was not a confronter or activist like those brave troops and protestors. Although I wanted a better, fairer world like the marchers and protestors, I didn't dare to join in their march for change and take the abuse they did. I just wanted to live a peaceful, simple life, raise my family, and be happy. I thought of the young man, full of hate, a complete stranger who had threatened me with a knife, and racist Cade from the agency with his hateful words and opinions. I realized the two of them, and others like them, would never set aside their strong prejudices against another race and be friends. They were locked in their positions as if carved from granite. They would never smooth or weather, no matter how life rubbed them differently or storms shifted their foundations. Perhaps life would be different for their children, and they would have a better understanding of others, but that seemed an elusive possibility far into the future.

I heard the whir of an air conditioner come on. Someone heavy-footed walked loudly around upstairs. Doors opened and closed, and I could hear the noise of the latch as cold metal met cold metal. The plumbing made rushing, watery noises as someone flushed a toilet. Muffled conversations, plus a noisy television, pierced the dark elsewhere. Someone's small dog yelped high-pitched barks in their apartment, and the owner screamed, "Shut up, goddammit!" Outside, an ambulance's high-pitched noise came closer and then faded away as it traveled on to its emergency. And, always, always every few minutes, the constant low, dull, continuous sound of jets arriving and taking off from Kennedy airport, just minutes apart, rumbled overhead in the sky day and night.

A wave of homesickness came over me that would have knocked me down if I were standing. I wanted to open my window like I used to do on a warm night and hear the wind rustling the aspen leaves on the trees. I wanted to hear crickets chirping to their mates in the dark as they clutched a tuft of hay. I needed to see the moon and stars in a full night sky and see the Big Dipper shining above me and the hundreds of twinkling blinks from lightning bugs dancing over the green timothy grass in the fields. My heart longed for the scent of life in those fields full of clover, buttercups, daisies, and wild strawberries coming to me through the open window screens. The deer mice and birds were sleeping, snuggled in their warm hay nests there. Lester's sheep would be baaing to each other as they stirred in their pastured sleep. I longed to hear an owl far off in the woods asking, "Whoo cooks for you, whoo cooks for you," the sound of his query traveling far in the stillness of the quiet country night. From the deepness of the woods, it floated on the gentle evening breeze to my open window, begging me for an answer to his question.

Then I thought that maybe our children would not benefit from living in this multicultural, cosmopolitan world of Washington, DC. We had believed it would be full of wonderful opportunities. But so many people bitterly distrust and dislike each other here. Our government was based there, and some of its deceitful leaders were lying to us about deadly critical issues like the Vietnam War. And many of those leaders were not the best options to represent and be advocates for the American people. They were not even the type I wanted to be around. There was so much crime and danger there. Way too much. I was afraid to leave my apartment to go to work. Even lying in the dark with that damn metal door and the three locks on it I did not feel safe. And I was so afraid for my children and their future now.

People born and raised in this city probably took all this chaos for granted in their daily lives. They probably thought it was what it had always been and always would be, so they didn't expect anything different. Perhaps these people of all races didn't even know daily life and interactions with others could be so different, so much better, so peaceful, so full of wonderful opportunities. Like the limited Amish woman Hope and I had talked about. How could they miss something they never knew existed or had never experienced?

But I knew.

I knew there could be a better life for the people living in this district and in Maryland, and I knew there could be a better life for my family. Then I asked myself, shouldn't we shelter our children from this place of chaos, deception, danger, and hate? It was a place where racism was the practiced norm and happened every day.

I remembered a saying Samuel's mother often repeated: "You can't catch what you aren't exposed to." And I realized I did not want my children to be exposed to all this terrible prejudice and "catch" it too. I knew my answer had to be "yes." We must get away from this city, this area, and its surroundings. Maybe someday, when our children were adults, they too may want to know what it's like to live in a big city instead of the country, and they could choose to do so then. They wouldn't have to grow up so fast if they didn't live near DC and could enjoy the freedom of being innocent children, playing outside, wandering the fields and woods, or being out after dark like Samuel and I had. I was fairly sure it was different in other parts of Maryland, where life might be more normal, more what we knew, and people felt more secure. But that was not the case where we lived now. Then I thought, *our children don't need to be a small part of a big cosmopolitan world like DC but can be a big part of a small country world instead.*

I wanted to go home. Home where I could feel safe again, shopping at the local grocery store anytime I wanted to, even after dark, with the clerks I knew and they knew me. I wanted to see familiar faces. I wanted my children to take long, bumpy bus rides over dirt roads to school with their friends past century-old dairy farms, where families had worked for many generations. At school, they would be with the children of my old school friends or neighbors. They could participate in a concert at our small school like we did, where all the grades stood tall on bleachers and sang out "God Bless America" as loud as they could, with the audience of parents and grandparents singing right along with them. I wanted my children to grow up where they were not hated, judged, or carried decades of racial baggage weighing them down because of their heritage. Many of the people of DC lived in fear and faced danger day and night everywhere because of their different skin colors.

I wanted to go to our country fair back home and see 4-H displays and blue ribbons on prize-winning livestock. And it was silly, but I wanted to check the newspaper obituaries at home for someone I might know and see flashbacks to times our paths had crossed and feel the connection with their family as a lost part of our community.

I thought about something Thoreau had written. It was, "I would rather sit on a pumpkin and have it all to myself than be crowded on a velvet cushion." I decided at that moment, lying there in the dark, that living a good life was more than chasing a prestigious job for higher income or a title as Samuel and I were doing now. People climbing the ladder for luxuries or status are just checking off all the "to-do" details of that day to make some more dollars and then repeating the same thing, day after day, postponing real happiness for later in life just to make more dollars.

When people talked about success back home, it wasn't measured by how much money you were making, or what fancy home you lived in, or the new car you drove. Instead, it was measured by how your kids did in school or what was happening at Little League, soccer, church, or scouts. Life was about finding a place where you fit into the space around you like a cozy, comfortable old bathrobe you wanted to wrap around you. A place where you were surrounded by people you knew cared about you and people you loved.

Life shouldn't be something you have to constantly adjust or repair or pile on more insulation or locks on heavy doors to protect you. Life should be an easy, open place that gives you enough peace and happiness that you can sleep at night without worrying about surviving the next day, even if you aren't wealthy. It should be a place that nourishes you. I wanted that for everyone, but most of all, I wanted our children's lives to have that kind of peace and security surrounding them. Things that we could count on to be there again, year after year. And I wanted their life to be full of opportunity.

I missed the hills, the woods, the wildflowers, the fields, the wild berry bushes I picked from, the songbirds, the big sky full of stars, the clear, sparkling, stony creeks that ran frigid even in August that no high rise would ever overshadow or pollute. I missed it all. I even missed a heavy snowfall covering everything with white and making the landscape look brand new. I fell asleep dreaming of home. The next morning, Samuel and I had a long, serious talk before he left for work. Together we made a decision.

We were leaving.

"What's going to happen to the United States, Samuel?" I asked him. "It seems so torn apart, so conflicted right now. There are so many people with agendas and demands, and many others are just butting their heads against someone else trying to force their will or agenda on the other."

"I don't know, Josey. I hope our country survives all this division and learns to take care of each other and work together," he said. "We're all like one big family, only on a much larger scale. We have some crazy uncles and aunts in the country, and some who break the laws or rules. There's always a good role model who reaches out and helps others and someone who's goofy funny and a joy to be around. Somebody will be really smart, and we can learn from them, and someone will be dumb as a rock and have no clue what the heck is going on. People will be needy and unable to survive without help, and another individual will give their life for people they don't even know or fight for justice for them. We have protectors who work to keep us safe and some leaders to help us keep democracy in our government. We have teachers and nurturers and people who give us spiritual guidance in our big family too."

Samuel continued: "There are people who strive for perfection in their soul, mind, body, or occupation, and people that just strive to make it through each day. That's the population of our country, our big American family. When I think about my own family with all my aunts and uncles and cousins plus yours, Josey, I could probably put one of those labels on each one of them. And when you think about it, we're all immigrants from different countries learning to be Americans and understand each other for the good of the whole family. Unless you're a Native American, your people came from someplace else, and that's most of the United States. This country is new despite the old appearing buildings in our capital that give the impression they've been here a long time. Like our children, our country hasn't finished growing into an adult yet. We have a history, but we still haven't written our future."

"Samuel, I don't want to be right in the middle of this terrible struggle and tension like we've been. I especially don't want our kids to feel hatred from anyone or be exposed to others that would teach them to be prejudiced and hate others. We have to adjust our dreams; we can't just work for a higher pay. Our children need something more important than that."

"I agree, Josey. I agree," Samuel said, sadly looking into my eyes and holding me close. He lifted my chin and spoke. "Today, I'm going to turn in my notice. My boss will be pissed. They spent a lot of time and money to give me more training, and we won't have much to move back on, but we'll survive. Hell, we survived being broke, leaving our home, changing jobs, and the riots, didn't we?"

We hugged tightly for a long moment and kissed goodbye when he left for work. I got some cardboard boxes from the storage area and started packing all our things. Once again, we made a difficult, life-altering decision and would upend our world. We were moving back home. We were giving up chasing that prestigious dream job, and earning a higher living for something more valuable, a happier and safer life for us all, but especially for our children.

# About the Author

DORIS WILBUR is the author of four novels: *A Lenape Legacy, Riding the Float, A Lenape Captive-Ahmeya,* and *Checkers on the Hill.* Her thought-provoking novels are based on historical events and concerning issues of contemporary times. They are infused with nature and detailed surroundings that give you a real sense of place while taking you on an engaging adventure filled with humor, romance, challenges, and accomplishments. Doris lives at a small private lake surrounded by the woods and wildlife she often includes in her novels. She has lived and worked in rural locations as well as large multicultural cities. She and her husband are proud parents of five children and now have a large, extended family. She graduated from Mansfield University where she studied Creative Writing, Art Education and Botany and graduated Summa Cum Laude. Her career has included being co-owner of a printing business, working as a commercial artist, and teaching in a public school. Now a senior, she has lived and worked in four different states and mines her years of experiences as produce for her engaging novels.

"Sometimes you leave home to find what you want
when what you wanted was there all the time,
and you just left it behind."

—ANON

THE END